Crest S

Copyright

Cover design by EDH Graphics

1. http://www.catcahill.com/

Chapter One

INDEPENDENCE, MISSOURI — May 1877

The billowing, white sails of the wagons almost made her change her mind.

Sophia Zane swallowed hard, her hand gripping the handles of her carpetbag. All that canvas, covering the wagons and rippling in the wind like clouds moving across an endless sky, reminded her of exactly where she'd be going if she didn't turn around right now.

The desolate West. Wide open. Dangerous. Alone.

Sophia glanced behind her at the road. If she turned around, she would be in familiar surroundings—but she would have nothing. And that was only if Mr. Durham saw fit to leave her alone after taking everything she had, instead of making her Mrs. Durham.

She closed her eyes and drew in a deep breath. She could do this. The money was her family's—hers alone now—not Mr. Durham's. Despite what his attorney had told her.

And she would use it to buy her way onboard one of these wagons, a far less expensive means of travel than the railroad.

Clutching her carpetbag to her as if it were the only thing keeping her from drowning in her own fear, Sophia forced herself to move toward the circled wagons. A woman with a kind face pointed her toward the wagon master.

"Pardon me, sir," she said to the man bent over the raised leg of his horse. Nearby, another man lay beside his wagon, pale and appearing to be ill.

The wagon master straightened, letting the horse's hoof return to the ground, and glanced from her face down to her carpetbag.

Sophia pushed a lock of hair from her face and opened her mouth to ask how much it might be to join a family on one of the wagons, but the man spoke first.

"Miss Daisy Timperman? You're late. We assumed you'd changed your mind. Find your party. We leave in the morning."

Sophia blinked at him. He thought she was someone else. Someone who had already paid for her place here and . . . and hadn't arrived. She ought to tell him the truth, give him the name she'd already conjured up for this journey. But . . .

If this Miss Timperman chose not to come, what would it hurt to simply take her place? Sophia could save the money she'd intended to spend on travel to secure her future in . . . wherever it was this wagon train was going.

"Yes," she said before she could change her mind. "I . . . I don't suppose you could remind me of the name of the people with whom I am traveling?"

The wagon master looked at her as if she were simpleminded. She could hardly blame the man. Who paid the sum needed to travel west and then forgot the name of one's traveling party?

She gave him her most winning smile, and he shook his head and laughed a little.

"I believe you're with the Randalls. Husband and wife, third wagon to the left." He pointed in the correct direction.

Sophia thanked him and made her way toward their wagon. A young woman, not much older than Sophia herself, noticed her the second she approached.

"You must be Miss Timperman," she said with the friendliest smile Sophia had seen since her own mother had passed.

It caught her off-guard for a moment, and she paused as bittersweet memories of Mama flooded her mind. And she instantly felt guilty about pretending to be someone else. *Mama would understand*, she told herself, and she forced her legs to move toward the woman waiting for her.

"I am," she finally said. "It's a pleasure to meet you, Mrs. Randall."

"Well, come. Let's get you settled and then you can help me with supper." Mrs. Randall reached for Sophia's carpetbag. Sophia handed it over gratefully. The money was safely hidden in a secret pocket she'd sewn into her dress. It was heavy, but far preferable to risk of losing it in the carpetbag.

Mrs. Randall chatted amiably as they cooked over an open fire, and thankfully Sophia didn't have to fill in with much conversation of her own. Up and down the circle of wagons, Sophia spotted other women—and a few men on their own—doing the same. Just as they were finishing up, Mr. Randall arrived laden down with sacks and bundles wrapped in brown paper, which Sophia found out quickly were their last-minute supplies of food. Flour, beans, sugar, potatoes, cornmeal, and other things they would need to make last for weeks.

"The missus and I are taking the trail clear out to Oregon. Mr. James said you would be leaving us in Colorado," Mr. Randall said, clearly curious about why Sophia—or Daisy—would be going to Colorado.

Which would be easier to answer if Sophia were actually Daisy.

"Yes," she said. "I'm going to Colorado." And then she hoped he wouldn't press any further.

It must have satisfied his curiosity, because Mr. Randall went on to inform them that a man traveling on his own had fallen sick and would be remaining behind. That must have been the fellow Sophia had seen when she first arrived. He had looked terrible, and she hoped he would improve.

As they bedded down for the night with Sophia and Mrs. Randall in the wagon, and Mr. Randall sleeping outside to keep an eye on the horses, the entire wagon train grew quiet.

It wasn't long before Mrs. Randall's slow, steady breathing filled Sophia's ears. Yet she herself couldn't fall asleep.

As she laid there, looking overhead at the canvas above her, all she could think was that she'd never slept anywhere but at home. The home she had to abandon. It hadn't been much, just a little apartment, but once it had been filled with the voices and great love of her parents.

But they were gone now, leaving Sophia with only memories and the money they'd meticulously saved and invested for years and years. Money that Mr. Durham claimed was owed to him.

Sophia shivered under the warm quilt at the thought of that man. He would *never* see her parents' hard-earned funds. And she would certainly never marry him.

Instead, she would go to Colorado.

Colorado. Sophia turned the word over in her mind and tried to picture it. But all she knew of the place was a vague notion of mountains, Indians, and wide-open space. Whether any of that was true, Sophia didn't know. But right now, anywhere was better than Kansas City, and so Colorado it would be.

Mr. Durham would never find her there. She wondered if he were looking for her now. Her heart picked up pace at the thought. No, he wouldn't be alarmed just yet. If he'd stopped by today, she hoped he would simply think she was out, doing some shopping or visiting. By the time he figured out she was missing, the wagon train would be long gone. And he oughtn't have a clue that this was the journey she'd decided to take. She hadn't told a soul where she was going.

And even if he did figure it out, he wouldn't think to look for her as Daisy Timperman.

Guilt sidled up next to Sophia again. If Miss Timperman had already paid for her place here and didn't arrive, surely there wasn't anything wrong with Sophia taking it. No, the guilt she felt was because she was pretending to be someone she wasn't. Perhaps she ought to have confessed that she wasn't Miss Timperman and paid if Mr. James had asked her to.

But every penny counted, even with the amount Sophia had. She didn't know what might be awaiting her in Colorado. That money could be used to pay for an apartment or for a room in a boarding house. For food, clothing, and other necessities that she'd had to leave behind.

If Sophia knew anything, it was that money meant security. And for a woman on her own, security was everything.

That money would keep her safe in an unknown place. She tried not to think too much on the *unknown* part. Surely

Colorado had a few established towns that would be safe for a young woman to live. Perhaps she might eventually meet a good man and have a family of her own, something she'd hoped to do in Kansas City before her parents' illnesses had required all of her time.

Sophia snuggled down under the quilt. She said a quick prayer for forgiveness for her lies about being Miss Timperman. And then she pushed away the fears, worries, and guilt at deceiving Mr. James and the Randalls. She filled up that space with thoughts about her new life to come—lovely, tall mountains, a nice little room, and a handsome gentleman looking for a girl just like her.

Chapter Two

PUEBLO, COLORADO — August 1877

The wagon train arrived three weeks late.

The news reached Matthew Canton as he took supper at the boarding house for the twenty-second day in a row. He had exactly enough money for three more days in Pueblo.

He left his meal half-eaten, tossed on his jacket, and grabbed his hat as he ran out the boarding house door and down to the Arkansas River where the wagon train was supposed to make camp before departing to follow the trail north.

It was easy to spot with all the white canvas and the smoke of multiple campfires reaching toward the sky. During his weeks of waiting, fear had begun to displace the nerves Matthew had felt about finally meeting Miss Timperman. According to the folks in Pueblo, wagon trains were delayed all the time because of weather, illness, lame animals, or any number of other things. But as one week turned into two, and two turned into three, Matthew began to worry.

What if it never arrived at all? What if some terrible fate had befallen Miss Timperman? Matthew thought he would never forgive himself if it was the latter.

After months of correspondence with the woman who was to be his mail-order bride, it was his idea to have her come by wagon. It was far less expensive than cross-country train fare. And that was money saved that they could then use to build a home on the land he'd purchased. Miss Timperman had agreed that this was a very sensible idea, and so he'd paid for her to travel with a young couple in their wagon.

But as he reached the circled wagons, he knew something was wrong.

It was in the air—a tense, scared feeling. Women walked together, talking in hushed tones, while the men stood in tight circles with drawn looks and arms crossed. The undertaker's horses and wagon stood nearby, and as Matthew approached, two men carried something that resembled a body wrapped in white toward the waiting wagon.

A disconcerting chill traced its way up Matthew's spine as he said a quick prayer under his breath for the deceased. And then another one asking for Miss Timperman's safety. He could almost hear one of his father's sermons in his head, telling him to have faith and be courageous.

Matthew adjusted his hat and surveyed the wagons, trying to decide the best way to go about finding his intended. He walked along the inside of the circle, pausing when he came across a woman placing a pot over a campfire.

"Pardon me, miss," he said, removing his hat. "I'm looking for a Miss Daisy Timperman. Do you know where I might find her?"

The woman's eyes widened slightly and she bit her lip. Without saying a word, she pointed across the circle.

Matthew turned—and saw a small group crowded around one wagon. He glanced back at the woman.

She gave him such a look of compassion that Matthew's heart seemed to fall right down into his boots.

"Thank you," he managed to whisper before running across the sage-covered ground.

He stopped just beside the group. A woman was in tears as a man Matthew presumed was her husband placed an arm around her.

"Thank you, Mrs. Randall," another man said. A silver star pinned to his vest caught the sunlight, and Matthew swallowed.

The county sheriff was here. Something had happened. Something bad. The sooner Matthew found his bride-to-be, the better he'd feel about all of this.

"Please find her," the woman with tears in her eyes said. "Daisy is a kind girl, and so very brave, and I don't— I don't—" She turned her face against her husband's chest again as she squeezed her eyes shut.

Matthew froze. *Daisy*. She'd said Daisy.

"We'll do our best, ma'am," the sheriff said. He began to walk away, another man at his side.

Matthew lurched into motion. "Sheriff!"

The men turned.

"Were you speaking of Miss Timperman?" He held out a sliver of hope that perhaps they'd meant another woman named Daisy.

"We were," the sheriff replied. "Are you acquainted with her?"

"No . . . Yes . . ." Matthew swallowed, trying to clear his head. "What I mean is that we were to be married upon her arrival." He glanced back at the couple near the wagon. The woman was wiping tears from her eyes, and all sorts of terrible scenarios ran through Matthew's mind. He turned back to the two men before him. "I've only just arrived. Please, tell me what's happened?"

The sheriff's face softened. He took off his hat and slapped it against his leg. "I'm very sorry, Mr. . . .?"

"Canton."

"Mr. Canton. I'm Edward Stone, county sheriff." The older man held out his hand. Matthew took it. He barely heard Sheriff Stone introduce his deputy. How could something have happened to Miss Timperman? Why hadn't he simply parted with the money for train fare? She'd be safe, and they'd be married already and back home in Crest Stone, making plans to build a home.

"I fear these wagons were attacked by road agents somewhere between here and Otero," Sheriff Stone said. "They made off with money and weapons, and after a few of the men from the wagon train tried to waylay them and prevent them from leaving, the outlaws shot a couple of them and took a woman with them to ensure no one would think of coming after them again."

"Miss Timperman?" Matthew could barely say her name. She must have been terrified. And it was all his fault.

"Yes, sir. I'm sorry to say it was her they took. Apparently they wanted Mrs. Randall over there, but your intended insisted they take her instead. Mighty brave woman, I'd say." The sheriff replaced his hat and glanced toward a group of men gathered off to the right.

"Yes, I suppose she is." Matthew said the words as his mind raced. If Miss Timperman was in danger, it was his duty to rescue her. "I'll go with you. I've got a horse over at the livery."

"Go with us?" Sheriff Stone furrowed his brow.

"To find Miss Timperman. I can be ready in just a few minutes. I owe that much to her."

The sheriff pressed his lips together. "Son, I can't spare the men for that."

Matthew stared at him, his mind trying to make sense of the sheriff's words. "You told Mrs. Randall you'd find Miss Timperman."

"I said I'd do my best. But it's going to be at least a week. Right now, I've got too much to handle here in Pueblo, and I've got men off looking for rustlers. I don't have enough men to spare. Besides, sounds like this happened in Bent County. I'll send a telegram to the sheriff over there. Now, if you'll excuse me, Mr. Canton."

Matthew stood, slack-jawed, watching as they left. His hands balled into fists at his sides. A *week*? He would not sit idly by for a week or wait for the sheriff elsewhere and hope Miss Timperman would be found safely.

If Sheriff Stone wouldn't help, he'd go find her himself.

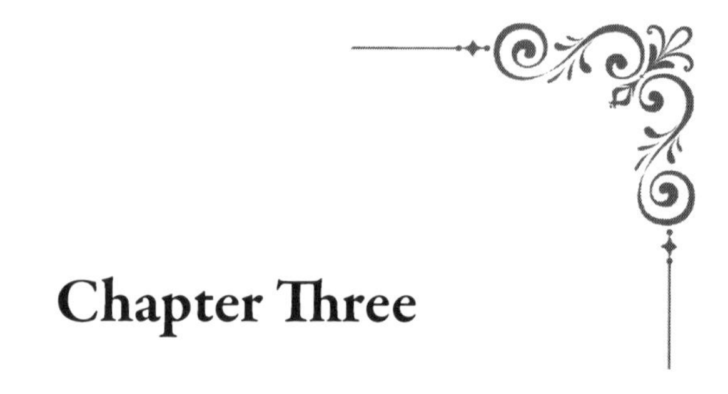

Chapter Three

WELL, THIS WAS SOME pickle she'd gotten herself into.

Sophia propped her chin with a hand on her knees as she watched the outlaws fuss over who had burned the beans. Which, she supposed, was better than listening to them argue over what they were going to do with her. Their suggestions ranged from the terrifying—leave her here alone in the desert to find her own way—to the horrifying—leave her here but tie her to the nearest tree.

She tried to focus on the good things. After four days, she'd convinced them to leave her hands free, and the chafing the ropes had caused was nearly gone. They'd fed her. It was awful food, but it *was* food. None of them had taken advantage of her, thanks to the oldest one, a fatherly sort who'd set any of the others straight with a good smack across the face for looking at her wrong. If they had, she would use that little knife Mr. Randall had slipped into her hand after she'd volunteered to take his wife's place. The one that was too small to scare them but big enough to do damage if her life was threatened.

But best of all, they were beginning to trust her not to run off, which worked in her favor.

Of course, it might help if there were anywhere to run *toward*. Or a tree or a hill or anything that might provide concealment. But the only things out here in this desolate corner of Colorado were bushy, silvery-green plants that Mr. James, the wagon master, had told her were sagebrush, sparse bits of other greenery, and miles upon miles of sandy dirt. Unless she could shrink herself to the size of a mouse, none of that would do her any good in an attempt to escape.

And so she sat here. And waited. And prayed they would either let her go near a town or that someone would eventually come to her rescue.

The wagon train had to have reached the next town by now. Perhaps there were lawmen searching for her right at this moment. Sophia held onto that hope with every fiber of her being.

"Here." One of the outlaws, a man the others referred to as Snake, held out the usual battered metal bowl with no fork or spoon. He and the older man, Roberts, appeared to be the ones in charge.

Sophia thanked him and slurped down the charred tasting beans. But instead of returning to the group around the fire, he stood there and watched her, his brow furrowed.

She forced herself to swallow as her heart began to thump harder. Why was he looking at her? She wiped her mouth with her hand, a terrible habit she'd grown used to over the past week. Had they made some decision about her fate?

"You know what I've been wondering?" he finally said.

Sophia shook her head, hoping it wasn't anything that would make him want to truss her up and leave her out here to die.

He crooked up the corner of his mouth, as if his own thoughts amused him. "Why a pretty young girl like you was traveling alone."

Sophia tried to ignore her racing heart. They didn't speak to her often, and then it was usually only to threaten her or ask if she needed to use the necessary. She took a deep breath, hoping it would steady her words. "I wasn't alone. I was with the Randalls."

He glanced behind him at the men, who had all paused in their eating to listen to the conversation. "Not what I meant. They were too young to be your parents and you weren't with a husband."

Sophia's stomach turned. Was he trying to find out if anyone would miss her? If they left her out here—or shot her outright—would anyone come looking for her?

Her heart sunk as she realized that no one would.

But this man didn't need to know that.

"That's because my intended is waiting for me to arrive." She paused, trying to determine how far she should push the falsehood she was spinning. "He's likely wondering where I am, if he hasn't already discovered what has happened."

Snake's expression changed. The lilt of his chilling grin fell away into a frown. "Your intended is in Pueblo?"

"He is." She said it before she could think through the fact that she didn't know where Pueblo was, much less whether it would be feasible for Miss Timperman's made-up fiancé to be living there.

But she liked the look of concern Snake gave Roberts, who stood, abandoning his bowl of blackened beans, to come join them. Roberts whispered something into Snake's ear as he rested a hand on the pistol in his holster. As protective as the older man had been toward her, he was the one who'd shot two of the men who'd tried to come after them when they left the wagon train the first time.

Before they'd grabbed Mrs. Randall, and before Sophia had offered herself. No one knew that Mrs. Randall had just discovered she was with child, but she'd told Sophia. And Sophia couldn't live with herself if she'd just let these outlaws take her.

Whether the two men he'd shot had lived or died, Sophia didn't know. But she knew he clearly didn't concern himself with the morality of killing a person.

"I imagine he's already looking for me," she said, desperate to prevent Roberts from convincing Snake to let him pull that revolver. "He's . . . he's well-connected in town with several friends. I'm certain they'd all be willing to help him."

They both looked at her now, and the men around the campfire remained silent. It was so quiet, Sophia thought they all could hear the pounding of her heart.

"Your man," Roberts said. "He's a . . .?"

She winced inwardly at needing to expand the lie even further. "A businessman. He runs a . . . business. He's very successful." She hoped they wouldn't ask what sort of business, because who knew what sorts of enterprises existed in Pueblo.

If there were any at all.

Sophia forced her expression to remain neutral even as her mind whirled. What if Pueblo was but a speck upon the desert? What if the only business there was a lodging house for weary travelers? Or a saloon?

Roberts glanced at Snake. They seemed to hold some silent conversation between them before Snake turned his gaze back toward Sophia.

"And your forthcoming marriage is a certainty?" he asked.

"Of course it is. Do you suppose I'd journey clear out here when I could have remained in Missouri if it wasn't?" She tried to sound indignant. As if she were some lucky bride on her way to marry the wealthiest man around instead of a girl simply trying to escape a greedy man with no plans beyond getting out of his reach.

They looked at each other again and Roberts nodded. "Javier," he suddenly shouted toward the men at the campfire. "Get me that pencil of yours. And some paper."

The dark-haired man who was always sketching leapt up and went to his saddlebags. He extracted the nub of a pencil and a crumpled piece of brown paper, like the kind one might wrap a parcel in for safekeeping. He handed it to Roberts, who held it out to Snake.

Snake crouched down and set the paper on his knee, paused a moment, and then began writing.

The minutes ticked by. A trickle of perspiration ran down Sophia's face, and she wiped it away. Finally, she could withhold her curiosity no longer. "What are you writing?"

Snake grinned, wrote a bit more before finishing with a little flourish, and held the paper out to read aloud. "Dear Sir, Please forgive this intrusion upon your daily affairs, but we thought you might like to know that we have your bride. She is well and safe and will remain so provided you part with the sum listed below. You may bring the money to the old fort south of Pueblo in two days' time. Come alone. Failure to heed this message and its instructions will result in Miss Timperman's life coming to an early and tragic halt."

Sophia sucked in a breath. Ransom. They were going to ransom her to the husband she'd invented.

"That's mighty eloquent," Roberts said. "Makes me wish I'd finished my own schooling."

Snake smiled before casting a glance at Sophia. "What's his name?"

She swallowed hard. A name. They needed a name. For the man who didn't exist. For the man who wasn't coming to rescue her. "Pollard," she finally said, borrowing the name of a neighbor she'd had growing up. "Seth Pollard."

"Hopkins." Snake thrust the note out to the pale, blond man who answered his call. "Ride fast up to Pueblo and deliver this to a Seth Pollard. Ask around till you find him. Then get out as quick as you can."

Hopkins nodded, shoved the note into his pocket, and went to saddle his horse.

Snake turned back to Sophia. "Thank you, Miss Timperman. You're about to make us very rich men."

Sophia forced a smile upon her face. They needed to think she was happy at the thought of being released. But the second he and Roberts returned to the campfire, her mind shot into action.

She had to get away. Tonight, maybe, or tomorrow night. Before they learned Seth Pollard didn't exist.

Before they figured out no one at all waited for her or cared if she was found.

Before they chose to relieve themselves of their burden and shoot her.

Chapter Four

THE MORE DESERT MATTHEW saw, the more he craved a return to the mountains. But he refused to leave unless Miss Timperman was at his side.

He was beginning to worry that would never happen. The food he'd carried was running perilously low, and he'd left the river behind to venture farther out into the desert. Father had often spoken of the trials one must face, like that of Jesus going into the desert. But Matthew had never imagined he would *literally* be in the desert. One thing was for certain—he wouldn't last forty days and forty nights out here.

They couldn't have gone too far from the river themselves, else they'd risk running out of water. With that thought in mind, Matthew decided he'd headed far enough south and turned toward the west, leading the horse he'd brought for Miss Timperman behind his own mount.

And that's when he found them. Or, rather, they found him.

He'd crested a rise and run straight into their guns, pointed directly at him. He'd seen his share of angry men, growing up on the edges of the frontier. They'd looked the same, no matter whether they were in Kansas or Montana or Colorado. The scowling faces, the quick reach for a gun or a knife, and the distrust that rolled off them in waves.

But these angry men had Miss Timperman.

He raised his hands as his gaze landed on her. She sat behind them on a horse. She looked unharmed, thankfully, although they'd tied her hands to her saddle. It was such a relief to see her. Although it *was* odd—he thought she'd described herself as having light-colored hair—

"Who are you?" the man in the front demanded. He looked to be just somewhat older than Matthew himself, not yet thirty, although living under the harshness of the sun had already begun to create lines on his forehead. His wheat-colored hair stuck out from under a hat that looked to have once been the shade of cream. And his scowl rivaled that of a drunken man who'd robbed Matthew outside a saloon back in Montana.

"Matthew Canton," he said, trying not to let his voice betray the nerves anyone would feel when having multiple weapons pointed at him.

"You alone?" An older man, one with an even more weathered face and dark hair shot through with gray, sauntered up on horseback next to the younger one. He glanced past Matthew as if he expected to see an army of men arising in the distance.

"Yes."

The man gestured at Matthew to throw down the revolver at his hip. He complied—and hoped his words alone would be enough to free Miss Timperman.

"Keep your hands where I can see them," the younger man said. "You run, I shoot."

Matthew nodded and rested his hands on the saddle horn.

"Why are you here?"

It was best to get straight to the point. "I've come for my intended." He nodded toward Miss Timperman, who stared at him as if she couldn't believe he'd come.

The older man raised his eyebrows while the blond one narrowed his gaze at Matthew. "Try that again."

"I've come to collect the woman I plan to marry. Miss Daisy Timperman. The lady you took from the wagon train." Matthew said it more slowly this time as he gestured toward Miss Timperman.

The two men looked at each other, as if they still couldn't understand what Matthew had said. The older one motioned for the man holding Miss Timperman's reins to bring her forward. And as the man did what was asked, Matthew finally got a good look at the woman with whom he'd been corresponding—the one who had agreed to come to Colorado to marry him.

And he wondered what Miss Timperman thought she saw when she looked in the glass at her home in Missouri. She was certainly pretty—beautiful even, Matthew thought—but not a thing like she'd described. Waves of dark hair—not blonde—that had fallen from pins framed her face, soft brown eyes instead of green, a pointed chin instead of a round face. Had he misread?

Or . . . a rock settled in his stomach at the thought. Had she been untruthful?

But why? That made no sense, when her true appearance was hardly one that any man could easily look away from.

"Did you receive the note?" the older man asked him.

Matthew tore his eyes away from Miss Timperman, who watched him with a guarded expression. "A note? I received no communication."

The older fellow made an incredulous noise in the back of his throat as the younger one leaned forward in the saddle to better see Miss Timperman. "I don't suppose the lady would care to explain to us all what's going on here?"

Miss Timperman pressed trembling pink lips together, and all Matthew wanted to do was grab hold of her and get her away from these men as fast as possible. The color of her hair and the shape of her face mattered not at all to him.

"This is the man I've come to marry." She hesitated, her eyes going from Matthew to the two outlaws. "I'm sorry," she said in a softer voice, one that just covered the terror hiding beneath. She swallowed before continuing. "I . . . I feared you might hurt him, so I gave a false name for him. He must have begun to worry over me and came looking."

Matthew thought he saw the older man's hand tighten around his pistol as he glanced back to his partner. The younger fellow's gaze traced Matthew, from his worn boots to his dusty coat to the hat that was in dire need of replacement. The man smiled without a trace of friendliness.

"I don't suppose you're a businessman?" he asked.

Matthew glanced at Miss Timperman. She knew of his work at the land office, as well as his intentions to begin ranching the land he'd purchased. Although he supposed that the land office *was* a business, and he did work there for now. That did make him a businessman of sorts, he supposed. "I work at the land office."

The blond outlaw downright scowled at Miss Timperman this time, and Matthew wondered what exactly he'd said to cause that response. She seemed to shrink into the saddle. Matthew gripped his horse's reins. How much had these men scared her already? He wanted to toss them both from their horses, grab her, and take her to where no one would ever harm her again.

"You and I have a very different understanding of *successful*," the younger outlaw fairly growled at Miss Timperman. When she didn't answer, he shot his gaze back to his companion, who shook his head.

"Leave it be, Snake. Let's cut our losses," the older man said.

After casting an angry look at both Matthew and then Miss Timperman, Snake—a well-earned name if Matthew had ever heard one—finally nodded.

"What've you got?" the older man asked. When Matthew didn't answer right away, he added, "For the lady."

Money. They wanted a ransom. His heart took a dive down to his boots. He didn't have much, not after three weeks at a boardinghouse in Pueblo, but perhaps they'd be satisfied with the little he had. "May I?" He pointed to his pocket.

When the older man gave a quick nod, Matthew reached into his pocket and extracted the paltry sum he had remaining. Snake urged his horse forward and held out his hand. Matthew dropped the bills and coins into it.

The man counted them silently and frowned. "That's all you've got?" When Matthew nodded, Snake glanced back at his companion. "Not even enough to buy a horse."

Matthew bit back his real thoughts—that they'd taken enough horses from the wagon train. Why would they need to bother with buying one?

"What else have you got?" the older man asked as Snake shoved Matthew's money into his own pocket.

The only other thing of value he carried, besides the horses, was the ring he'd planned to give Miss Timperman. He'd hoped they could be married by his father, back in Crest Stone, but he'd also planned for a hasty wedding in Pueblo if she didn't relish the idea of riding back home with him unwed.

It hurt to lose the ring, but he'd give up that slim band of gold for her life over and again. "I have a ring in my saddlebag. A marriage band made of gold."

Miss Timperman's eyes widened, and Matthew hoped she knew he'd work his fingers to the bone to buy her another one. When Snake held out his hand, Matthew dismounted and extracted the ring from the saddlebag.

"We'll take the horses too," the older man said. "Both of them."

Matthew ground his teeth to keep from telling them exactly what he thought about that. Drawing in a breath, he tempered his emotions and then said, "You may have mine. The other one is for the lady. Surely you don't expect her to walk all the way back to Pueblo?" Or to Crest Stone, but if Miss Timperman hadn't mentioned the name of the town where they planned to live, Matthew wasn't about to share that information with these men.

"She has legs, doesn't she?" Snake replied with an irritated laugh. "Both horses. Collins!" he shouted to one of the men behind him.

The man Matthew presumed was Collins rode forward and took the reins of Matthew's horse, along with the one he'd brought for Miss Timperman.

He didn't want to know how much he was going to owe the livery in Crest Stone for two lost horses. But that wasn't something he could think on now, considering the older man was eying him in a way that made Matthew feel as if he weren't done taking yet.

"I have nothing left," Matthew said, holding out his empty hands. "Not even a canteen."

"Seems like it's not much for the life of this woman you claim you want to marry," the man called Snake said. He turned to the older outlaw. "I say we keep her."

Anger blazed through Matthew. He'd taken one step forward when Miss Timperman spoke.

"I have money."

Every gaze turned toward her. Matthew prayed this wasn't another of her stretched truths. Even if it were meant to save them, he couldn't fathom how lying about having money one couldn't produce could be at all helpful.

She leaned down, pulled at a seam on her skirt until it must have given way, and yanked out a wad of bills.

They all stared at her another moment, Matthew in as much surprise as the outlaws. She shook the money, as if she were impatient for them to take it.

Had she a dowry she hadn't mentioned? Or had she sold something dear and valuable? His questions went unanswered as Snake urged his horse forward and snatched the lot from Miss Timperman's hand. He flipped through it quickly and handed it to his friend.

"You had that the entire time?" he asked, a laugh lurking at the edge of his voice.

She nodded and then lifted her chin. "It's more than enough. You don't want me slowing you down. May we go now?"

The older man lifted his eyes from the bills. "They can identify us."

"We're miles and miles from town. Considering we don't have horses, you can be long gone before we've even arrived," Matthew said.

"Besides," Miss Timperman added. "All I wish is to be married and to forget this ever happened. I don't much care where you go, so long as you never bother me—and my husband—again."

Matthew couldn't help the little smile that lifted the corners of his lips at his future wife's courage. From her letters, he'd never imagined Miss Timperman to be one to stare down a band of outlaws, much less volunteer to take another woman's place as their captive.

"They may not even make it back," Snake said. "If they don't find water."

The older man glanced at Snake, and then nodded. "All right." He tipped the brim of his hat toward Miss Timperman. "It's been a pleasure, miss."

"I won't say the same," she replied as she began to awkwardly dismount the horse with her tied hands. Matthew rushed to her side and grabbed hold of her waist before she fell backward into the sand and sage.

"Grab the horse," Snake called to one of the other men.

"Could one of you cut this rope?" Matthew asked, but the men had already begun riding away.

The last one grabbed hold of Miss Timperman's horse's reins. He paused, turned quickly to look at the others—none of whom were facing them—and then tossed his own canteen to the ground in front of them.

"Thank you," Miss Timperman said softly.

He gave her a smile and then followed the others, leading her horse behind them.

And leaving Matthew to forge his way through the desert with nothing but a canteen and the woman he was planning to marry.

Chapter Five

HOW HAD SHE WISHED a fiancé into being?

No, that was ridiculous. But how else could Sophia explain the presence of the man who was now pushing and pulling at the rope around her wrists?

And he wasn't just *any* man. He was exactly the sort Sophia might have chosen for herself, if she'd had time for suitors back in Kansas City. Tall and rugged, with a kind smile, he had rich brown hair that her mother would have said was a bit too long and dark blue eyes. Those eyes had darkened when he'd looked at the outlaws that had held her captive. She was certain he would have fought every single one of them for her freedom—and she'd never even met him before.

"Almost got it," he said through clenched teeth as he yanked on the rope.

Sophia waited silently. Thankfully, she'd caught his name when her captors had asked for it. *Matthew Canton*. It was a good name, strong and with purpose.

And one she knew belonged to Daisy Timperman—not to Sophia Zane.

He was the reason Daisy was supposed to be on that wagon train. And clearly, he'd never met Daisy or seen a photograph of her, else he'd know Sophia was an impostor. Which meant their marriage was some sort of arrangement. Through well-meaning relatives, perhaps, or through a church hoping to civilize the West with the presence of good women. Or maybe Daisy had answered an advertisement for a wife.

She must have changed her mind. Or else she'd gotten sick, or—heaven forbid—passed on. But one might think her family would have notified Mr. Canton of those latter two options. No, Daisy Timperman did not plan on marrying Mr. Canton.

Of course, Sophia was now Daisy. Which meant—

"There!" Mr. Canton held up the rope.

"Thank you," she said, rubbing her hands over her wrists to ease the raw ache.

He lifted the strap holding the canteen over his shoulder as he glanced out over the barren landscape. The dust the outlaws had stirred up as they left was now long gone, and it was just the two of them—and whatever else might live out here.

Daisy shivered with the notion. Sure, she'd survived several nights out here, but that had been with multiple men armed with shotguns and pistols. The bandits had taken Mr. Canton's revolver.

"It's late in the day," he said. "Which means that's north." He pointed in a direction that looked exactly the same as every other direction. "We'll eventually hit the river if we go that way, and we can follow that into Pueblo."

Sophia nodded, not having any better advice herself. And besides, it seemed as if Mr. Canton knew what he was doing, which was more than she could say for herself.

They walked a little ways in silence, and just as Sophia thought she might burst from the fear that he'd figure out she wasn't Miss Timperman and leave her here in anger, he finally spoke.

"I'm sorry I handed over the ring I bought you. Once we arrive in Crest Stone, I'll see about getting another."

She nodded, not sure what else to say.

"You do still wish to marry immediately?" His voice was laced with a hesitation that made Sophia's heart ache.

She didn't dare look at him. What if he could see her masquerade in her eyes? "I . . . Yes." She swallowed and tried to sound more decisive. "Yes, of course."

Out of the corner of her eye, she saw the faintest whisper of a smile cross his face. She'd made him happy, and for some reason, the thought made her heart swell.

"Only if you're certain. After all, you've been through a trial I daresay most women—or men—never face." He looked at her then, catching her eye before she could turn away.

Sophia forced herself to smile. Daisy would smile, after all. Because Daisy wouldn't be deceiving him and feeling as terrible as Sophia did about it. "It was terrifying," she said truthfully. "But they didn't hurt me."

He nodded, those blue eyes hardening just enough that Sophia knew her earlier thoughts had been correct. He would have taken on each one of those men if he discovered they'd hurt her at all.

She'd never seen that promise from anyone else, save perhaps from her own father.

It's not for you, she reminded herself. But it certainly felt nice to bask in the glow of his protectiveness.

"How . . . how did you find out where I was?" she asked, trying to force her mind away from thoughts of something that would never happen. She was Sophia Zane, a woman who had left with an inheritance her father's former business partner claimed was his. A woman he'd likely been tearing the city apart to find. A woman who'd pretended to be someone else to get away. She was certainly not Daisy Timperman, a sweet, unencumbered lady who'd made promises to marry.

"The wagon train finally arrived in Pueblo. When you weren't there, and I learned the sheriff was uninterested in looking for you—" He scowled at that. "I left to look for you on my own."

"And you found me," she said.

"It feels like a miracle." He gave her that warm smile again, the one that any woman might swoon over.

"A miracle," Sophia agreed. And although she was often given to doubt, it did seem like such a thing had occurred.

They walked in silence again, but this time it felt companionable rather than awkward. Sophia forced thoughts of what she'd do once they reached Pueblo from her mind. After all, she had plenty of time to worry on that. First, they had to survive this journey.

And she had to survive the guilt that gnawed at her insides.

She would tell him, she decided. Not right now, but soon.

But the decision made her frown. He wouldn't leave her here, no matter what. She was certain enough of his character, even after only knowing him half a day. He wasn't the sort to abandon a woman alone in the desert.

No, it was fear. She ought to have told him immediately, but that time had passed. She'd let him entertain thoughts of their marriage, and worse . . . she'd liked it.

It felt nice having someone who cared enough for her to do anything to keep her safe. Who looked at her as if she were the most precious thing on earth. Who wanted to love her.

Sophia swallowed the lump that grew in her throat.

Mr. Canton passed her the canteen, and she took one tiny, grateful sip.

"Tell me more about Harriet," he said after taking his own sip. "I enjoyed the stories in your letters."

Sophia froze. This was it. He'd figure it out when it became clear she didn't know who Harriet was, much less anything she'd supposedly written him.

He watched her now, waiting.

She had to say something. But what?

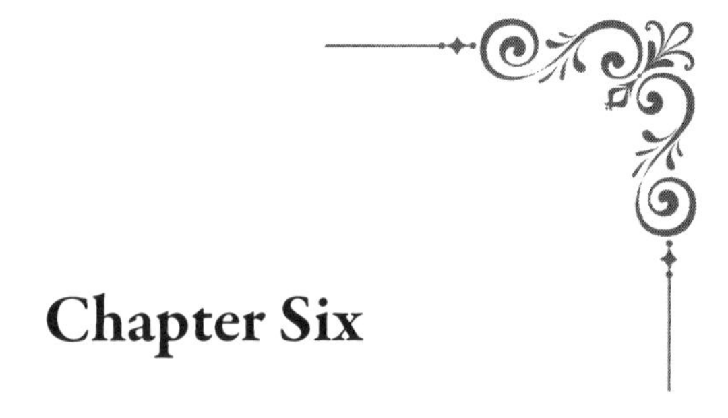

Chapter Six

"HARRIET." MISS TIMPERMAN looked straight ahead as she repeated her sister's name. There was a spark of hesitation in her voice, and Matthew hoped all was well with the younger Miss Timperman. "Well . . . which story of her did you enjoy the most?"

Matthew thought through the few she'd mentioned in the letters they'd exchanged. "The one with the rabbit. That one made me laugh so much I read it aloud to my parents."

She finally looked at him and smiled. "Harriet does so love rabbits."

Matthew tilted his head. If he remembered that story correctly, Harriet had run away from the wild rabbit outside their home. She was so frightened, she tripped right over the dog who had covered her face in kisses as Harriet was certain the rabbit would hop up and eat her alive. But that *had* happened some time ago, so perhaps . . . "She's changed her mind about them, then?"

"She . . . uh . . . well, yes." Miss Timperman glanced toward the ground, so quickly that Matthew wasn't certain if her cheeks had actually gone pink or if he'd imagined it. "Please forgive me. I'm tired, and I fear I won't be much of a storyteller at the moment."

"Of course." Matthew could have smacked himself. After all she'd been through, it was selfish of him to ask her to entertain him.

Off toward the west, the sun was beginning to sink, casting a glow that illuminated the mountains far off to the east. They wouldn't have daylight much longer. "Why don't we look for a place to make camp for the night?" he suggested.

She nodded, shooting him a grateful smile.

They walked on for a few more minutes before Matthew pointed out a lone tree. It wasn't much, but it was as good a place as any. He took off his coat and laid it down on the flattest piece of ground he could find and gestured to Miss Timperman to sit.

"Thank you," she said. "But what will you sleep on?"

"I'll be fine." He settled himself nearby, close enough to be of comfort—he hoped—but far enough away to keep her from thinking he was after anything untoward before their marriage.

Her stomach grumbled and she placed a hand over it. "I'm sorry."

"Don't be. I'm just as hungry. Tomorrow we'll try to make better time, and perhaps we'll arrive soon after that." Or so he hoped. He'd done more traveling east than south in his search for her, so they couldn't be too far away from the river. It was lack of water he worried about more than lack of food.

Keep faith. Matthew could hear his father's voice in his head as he opened the canteen and handed it to Miss Timperman. She took only a sip, and he was grateful she was a sensible woman. It was difficult to stop when one was so thirsty, but she must know they wouldn't make it to the river if they gulped the little water they had.

"We ought to get some sleep," he said as he laid back on the ground, knowing he wouldn't sleep much himself. Between the possibility of rattlesnakes and the outlaws changing their minds and returning, his mind would be too on edge to fall asleep for long.

What he would do if either of those possibilities—or any other just as heinous—came along, he didn't know. Never in his life had he wished so much for a weapon of some sort. Even a butter knife would give him at least a degree of comfort now.

Miss Timperson curled up on her side, facing him. Matthew tried to keep his eyes facing upward, toward the stars that were beginning to dot the sky, instead of staring at her.

"It looks the same here as it does everywhere," he said, more to distract himself from the way she looked to him to keep her safe than in actual admiration of the night sky. Although it *was* impressive, the thousands of pinpricks of light against the velvety black that would emerge after a while.

Miss Timperman turned to look up. "I don't know. It somehow seems bigger here. With more stars than I remember seeing in Kansas City."

Matthew frowned at the sky. She'd only been in Kansas City a short time, waiting to board the wagon train in Independence. "I would have thought they'd look the same at your farm," he said carefully.

She said nothing for a moment, and then, "No. Most certainly not the same."

He rolled over to face her. Something most definitely didn't add up. The hair color, Harriet and the rabbit, the farm, the money . . . He hadn't dared ask about the money. "Daisy," he said slowly. "May I call you Daisy? I feel as if we know each other very well from our letters."

"You may," she said. She didn't ask to call him Matthew in return.

He looked down at the arm he leaned on. He shouldn't do it. It felt wrong . . . Father would say it was wrong. But he opened his mouth anyway. "Remind me again of your middle name? I can't remember precisely. Was it Jane? Or June?"

"Yes, you're correct." She didn't bother saying *which* name was the right one.

And that was because Daisy's middle name was Sarah.

Matthew sat up, blood pounding in his ears. This woman beside him—the one he'd risked his life for—wasn't Daisy at all.

"Are you all right?" she asked, sitting up also.

Fear for the actual Daisy Timperman quickly doused his fury at being deceived. Where was she? What had happened to her?

"Who are you?" he finally asked as a million scenarios ran through his mind. "And where is the real Daisy Timperman?"

Chapter Seven

SOPHIA DUG HER FINGERS into the wool of Mr. Canton's coat. Her mind raced backward, picking apart every word she said—and finding a hundred different ways she'd given away the truth.

It's for the best. She repeated the words in her head and her grip loosened on the coat. She'd planned to tell him anyway . . . at some point. Swallowing, she held the glare he leveled at her. "I don't know where the real Miss Timperman is. I've never met her."

At that, he stood.

She scrambled up as he began to pace.

"Then how did you come to take her name? And who *are* you?" He threw the words at her as if they might hurt.

He likely did hurt, she realized. The woman he'd waited for wasn't here. She pressed her lips together. She hated to tell him the truth—it would only serve to hurt him more. But she couldn't abide any more lies.

The truth it would be, and she'd tell it as gently as she could.

"My name is Sophia Zane." She started softly, so quiet he had to stop pacing to hear her. "I'm from Kansas City. I arrived at the wagons the night before they were due to leave, ready to pay my way to ride along with a decent family. I . . . I needed to leave as soon as possible." Perhaps she'd tell him more about Mr. Durham later, if he didn't leave her here alone in the desert.

"The wagon master assumed I was Miss Timperman," Sophia continued. "Apparently she was the only person who hadn't arrived yet and they'd begun to think she wasn't coming. I ought to have corrected him, I know that. But it meant not having to pay, and if I could save that money to start anew somewhere out West, I'd be better off for it. So I went along with his assumption. If the real Miss Timperman had arrived, I would have stepped aside and paid to ride with another family. But she . . . she . . ."

What was the best way to tell a man as good and kindhearted as Mr. Canton that his intended had never come?

"She changed her mind." The words he said were devoid of emotion, as if he had to strip away his feelings in order to get them out of his mouth.

"I don't know if that's true," Sophia said as gently as possible. "Perhaps she fell ill."

His jaw worked as he rested his hands on his hips. "She would have written, or asked her mother to write, if she was unable." He glanced at her and Sophia nodded.

"It's what I would have done," she said. "Then again, I also would have felt the need to write if I'd had a change of heart." The thought of promising someone marriage and then changing one's mind without a word felt utterly cruel.

Mr. Canton nodded. And then, as if remembering he was supposed to be angry with her, he frowned. "Why didn't you say anything? Why did you let me believe you were her?"

Sophia's face went hot in the darkness. Well, if she were being truthful, she might as well continue. "At first, I feared you'd grow angry and leave me here. And then I . . ." She drew in a deep breath. "I didn't want to hurt you."

He blinked at her, disbelief coloring his features. "You didn't want to hurt me," he repeated.

She nodded. It sounded ridiculous, saying it aloud.

And then he did the thing she least expected—he laughed.

Sophia's eyes widened and she wrapped her arms around herself. Had he gone mad? Whatever in the world was so funny?

"I'm sorry," he said, his voice hoarse. "My fiancée didn't show up, you pretended to be her, and then you told me you were she—because you didn't want *me* to be hurt." He cocked his head. "Exactly how far were you planning to go with this farce? To the altar? To the birth of our first child? To death?"

Sophia wanted to shrink back at his words, but she forced herself to straighten her shoulders. Yes, she'd been wrong, but she confessed and she apologized. What more did he want from her? "I would have told you once we reached safety, probably."

"Probably?" He arched his eyebrows, but the pain still showed in his eyes and the tight way he held his jaw. And she knew then it wasn't from her pretending to be Daisy. It was from Daisy's rejection.

"I hated the thought of hurting you," she said, more quietly this time.

He closed his eyes, and all she wanted to do was to reach out and comfort him somehow. To lay a hand on his arm, to take one of his hands between both of hers—anything to try and make him feel better.

He dropped his hands from his hips and sat down abruptly. Sophia sank onto the ground beside him, her feet tucked beneath her. She wanted to say something, but she didn't know what. She wished Mama were here to whisper soothing words that Sophia could repeat. Perhaps if she just sat here, close enough so he knew he wasn't alone, that would be enough.

Mr. Canton rubbed his forehead with his hand, and when he looked up at her, the anger was gone, and all she could see was a man hollowed out by the loss of a great promise. "Why wouldn't she write?"

Sophia took a moment to think before she spoke, but no reason that wasn't cowardly came to mind. "I don't know," she said honestly. "She must have been afraid." *Or cruel*, but she didn't give those words life.

Mr. Canton shook his head. "I've made so many plans."

"Well . . ." Sophia moved her legs to the side as she looked for the hope to be found in the situation. "Surely she isn't the only woman looking for a better life who might take a chance on a young, handsome gentleman who works in a land office."

"Handsome?" He raised those eyebrows again, but this time they were accompanied by a little smile.

Heat rushed to Sophia's cheeks. She hadn't even realized she'd said the word. She wanted to look down and hide her face, but she forced herself not to. He needed to feel better about himself, and if that came with a little embarrassment on her part, she could handle that. "I may have pretended to be Miss Timperman to get here, Mr. Canton, but I assure you I don't craft lies as a daily exercise." She frowned a moment.

"Well, despite the fiancé I invented for those outlaws. But that was to save my own life, so I don't think that counts."

"You invented a fiancé?" He shook his head. "I oughtn't be surprised, although I suppose that explains their confusion at my name."

Sophia bit back a sigh. In his eyes, she was still a liar, someone who'd cheated her way onto a wagon train and then deceived him to escape a band of outlaws. "I didn't know Miss Timperman's intentions upon going West. And so when those outlaws seemed to be trying to find out if anyone would miss me if I never returned, well . . . I told them the story of a man waiting for me in Pueblo." She paused. "I didn't know that man was you."

He watched her, and she couldn't tell if he was curious, irritated, or what precisely. She couldn't bear it if he expressed disappointment in her again. She suddenly wanted him to know her as she'd been in Kansas City—a good, loyal daughter, a friend to anyone who needed someone, a caregiver with patience that rivaled that of those trained to care for the sick.

"I will help you find a wife." The words tumbled out before she could make sense of them. "Once we return. I'll help you."

Chapter Eight

MATTHEW STARED AT HER in disbelief. "You're coming to Crest Stone?"

"I suppose it's as good a place as any. Is it a nice town?"

"It's . . . yes," he said carefully. "It won't compare to Kansas City, and it has rough edges, but it's growing."

"Then I suppose it will do." She gave him a tentative smile as he tried to piece together the puzzle that was Miss Zane.

Putting aside her promise to help him find a wife—as unnecessary and unexpected as *that* was—he concentrated instead on the fact that she'd come all the way out here seemingly without a plan. "Did you not have a destination in mind?"

Miss Zane drew up her knees and rested her chin on them. "I didn't. My only thought was to leave Kansas City. Once I took Miss Timperman's place and discovered she was to leave the wagons in Colorado, I figured that would work out just fine."

Matthew couldn't find words for his thoughts. Did she not realize the danger that came with her journey? Did she expect to arrive in Colorado and simply find a decent man to marry? Or did she think it would be safe to live as a woman all alone in some frontier town?

Only one thing was clear—Miss Zane didn't know the first thing about the country into which she'd thrown herself.

She chewed on her lip as he stared at her. "Is it . . ." She paused and raised her head. "Is it all right if I come to Crest Stone with you?"

"I insist on it," he said before he realized the commitment he'd taken on. Liar or not, he could hardly abandon a young woman to fend for herself in Pueblo.

A smile brightened her face. "Thank you. And I promise I'll do the best I can to find a good woman to be your wife."

Where she planned to find one, Matthew didn't know. "There's a reason I employed an advertising service."

"Hmm. Well, in that case, I'll assist you with your letters."

He didn't dare tell her that writing and receiving letters was not something he necessarily needed help with. She seemed so eager to do something. Was it guilt for lying to him? Or was it simply part of her nature to want to help?

His mind was far too mixed up to think any more on it tonight. "We ought to get some rest."

She nodded and laid down. It wasn't long at all before her measured breathing indicated she'd fallen asleep, leaving Matthew alone with the thoughts spinning in his mind.

MATTHEW AWOKE AT DAWN, surprised to find he'd fallen asleep at all. He sat up and stretched muscles that ached beyond anything he'd ever felt before in his life.

Beside him, Miss Zane still slept, curled up on his coat. The cloud settled over his heart again. She wasn't Daisy Timperman. He wouldn't be arriving back in Crest Stone with a bride.

He had to start the search all over again. Thoughts tossed again through his mind, seeking out all the words he might have said in his letters that made Miss Timperman have a change of heart.

No. What was done, was done. It was good that she chose not to come at all, rather than arrive and then decide to leave. All he had now was wounded pride, which was preferable to a shattered heart.

Miss Zane stirred, and Matthew couldn't help but smile. He ought to still be angry with her. And to be honest, he wasn't *entirely* certain she was trustworthy. Time would tell whether her lies were as she'd said, desperate and situational, or more of a compulsive nature. But in the meantime, he was absolutely certain she was brave, smart, and well . . . pretty.

He shook his head and stood. Thoughts like that would only lead to trouble. He'd take her back to Crest Stone, and she could carve out a life there if she chose. There were more than enough men, if she wanted to marry, or plenty of new opportunities if she preferred to work in a store or a restaurant. She would be safer there than alone in some wilder place.

As for him, he'd comb through the other letters he'd received again. Perhaps one of them would strike his fancy now that Miss Timperman was no longer an option.

That thought felt like a long slog through mud. Matthew tried to push it from his mind as he took a small sip from the canteen. They had to reach the river today, or he'd be facing something a lot more terrible than choosing another woman to write to. His throat was parched with the small rations of water he'd had yesterday, and there was barely enough left in the canteen to sustain the both of them through the day.

With the need to get to the river in mind, he gently shook Miss Zane's shoulder until she awoke. She blinked at him with eyes as dark as chocolate as she pushed a strand of hair from her face. A tiny stab of disappointment sliced through Matthew at the fact that she was not Miss Timperman.

"Water?" He held out the canteen to distract himself from that line of thinking. She reached out a hand and he handed it to her. "Just a sip."

She dutifully drank only a little before returning the canteen to him. "I am awfully thirsty."

"I know." He slung the canteen over his shoulder. This was the first complaint she'd had, and it was hardly one at all. He could add *resilient* to the list of Miss Zane's attributes. "I am too. I'm hopeful we'll reach the river today if we start walking now."

She nodded and stood before bending over to pick up his coat. As she handed it to him, her face, still pink from yesterday's sun, went an even deeper shade of red.

She didn't need to ask, and he mentally berated himself for not offering to distance himself for a few minutes last night so she could attend to her needs. "I'll wait over there." Matthew pointed in a northerly direction.

Miss Zane nodded gratefully, and in a short time, she joined him and they were on their way again.

The walk was quieter today. As many questions as he had about Miss Zane, Matthew feared speaking would only make them both thirstier, and so he kept conversation to the minimal amount needed.

The day stretched on and on. Matthew kept an eye out for snakes, outlaws, and the welcome water of the Arkansas River.

He steered Miss Zane away from a rattler midafternoon, when the creature's telltale sound made him grab hold of her arm. She didn't protest, instead allowing him to lead her in a wide berth around the snake.

And when she said, "Thank you" in that melodic voice of hers, all his troubles felt as if they'd retreated toward the horizon. Only when he finally let go of her arm and tore his eyes from hers did they come rushing back—along with every shred of his sense.

He needed a woman who was honest, not one who had lied and schemed her way to Colorado. He would repeat that to himself as much as necessary, even as he questioned it.

Step after step, they continued through the sagebrush, spiky grasses, and sandy dirt, despite the rawness in their throats. Here and there, a cheerful wildflower poked its face up from the monotony, a reminder that there was hope still to be had. Matthew clung to that hope. He thought of his parents waiting back in Crest Stone, the land he'd purchased, his dreams of a ranch, his friends in town, and the woman at his side—the one who entrusted him to lead her to safety—and he kept going.

Late in the day, the glint of something bright nearly blinded him.

"What is that?" Miss Zane asked, holding a hand over her eyes to shade them from the sun that had begun its decline toward the western horizon.

Matthew stopped and squinted. It couldn't be . . . He almost didn't dare hope it was. And if anything, he didn't want to raise Miss Zane's hopes. "Let's find out."

She nodded, and from the way she held his gaze, he knew she understood. But the smile that crossed her face as she turned to look forward again was contagious, and he found himself grinning in anticipation of the cool, wet river that awaited them.

Chapter Nine

THEY REACHED THE RIVER in just under an hour. It was slow and sluggish at this time of year, and it rolled by them as if it didn't care at all about their arrival.

Sophia couldn't fall to her knees fast enough once they reached its banks. She cupped her hands, ready to fill them with that cold, wonderful water when Matthew laid a hand on her arm. She startled at the feel of his grip, strong and sure, just as it had been when he'd saved her from walking straight into that rattlesnake.

"Wait," he said. "We ought to boil it to keep from getting sick. But we have nothing to contain the water, and nothing with which to start a fire." His laugh was hollow. "I suppose that means we take our chances."

As much as Sophia wanted to thrust her face into the river and drink until thirst was a distant memory, she shook her head. She was nothing if not resourceful, and the last few months had proven exactly that. "Give me a moment."

Gathering her skirts, she rose and threaded her way through the tall grass at the river's edge, praying there were none of those snakes or any other venomous creatures lurking in the brush.

"What are you searching for?" Matthew asked at the same time her eyes landed on her prize.

"This!" She turned and held out a piece of wide driftwood, washed up by the river and with a perfect bowl-shaped indentation in the middle. Then she felt for the hidden pocket in her skirts, the one that still held what was left of her money—and the small knife Mr. Randall had given her. She'd shoved into the mostly stitched-up pocket before the outlaws noticed it. She pulled it out now and brandished it as if it were made of pure gold.

Matthew's eyes widened. "You've had that the entire time?"

"Yes." Sophia glanced at the knife. "I'm sorry. I know it would have made getting those ropes off a little easier, but I didn't know you then. I thought it smarter to keep this to myself."

Matthew shook his head, but he smiled. "All right. You have a bowl to scoop water, and a knife for . . . ?"

"Fire," she said triumphantly. "All I need are a few rocks. Dry and a few should be small enough to fit into this makeshift bowl." She looked down and eyed one of the perfect size and shape. "Like this one."

A few moments later, Matthew dumped a variety of rocks a few feet away from the bank, and Sophia got to work. Leaning over the little nest of dried twigs and dead grass she'd gathered, she struck the knife against the largest of the rocks.

"I remember my father doing that," Matthew said as Sophia struck the rock again. "Years ago, when we were on our way west from Illinois. I'd forgotten all about it. How did you learn?"

Sophia smiled as she hit the rock again. She'd impressed him. That was a start, at least. Perhaps that would eventually give way to respect, forgiveness, and, she hoped, trust.

And why exactly his opinion mattered so much to her, she couldn't put a finger on. Instead of trying to figure *that* out, she cast her smile up at him and said, "On the wagon train. Mrs. Randall showed me."

Matthew nodded, his approval written all over his face. Sophia turned her attention back to her work, and just as she was about to despair, sparks leapt from the rock. She hit it again, and those sparks caught fire. Then, very carefully, she leaned closer to the little flame and blew gently to encourage it to grow.

And grow it did. Before too long, she had a decent little fire. One by one, she set the smaller rocks into the flames, using the larger one to nudge them in without burning herself. Matthew settled himself next to her, watching intently—which was a good thing, because Sophia was certain her cheeks had gone pink again. She could have measured the distance between them in finger lengths. What was it about this man that made her feel overly aware of every movement she made?

"We'll heat these rocks, and then drop them into our bowl of water. If it works as I think it will, it'll set the water to boiling—"

"And we can drink it." The note of awe in Matthew's voice was unmistakable, and this time Sophia flushed with triumph. Now if only she could convince him that she was someone he could trust—and not a liar intent upon deceiving him.

Her plan worked just as she'd hoped, and it wasn't long before they were drinking as much water as they could hold.

It was time-consuming, going back and forth to the river and boiling another bowl of water, but Sophia thought it the best tasting water she'd ever had.

"I doubt any water will ever taste as good as this," Matthew said, echoing her thoughts.

"I'm equally as adept with a bowl of dough," Sophia said as they waited for another bowl to boil. "Biscuits, bread, pie crust, anything." The moment it was out of her mouth, she wished she could take the words back. He must think her the least humble woman he'd ever met.

But instead of looking irritated, Matthew smiled. "What I'd give for a biscuit or a cookie right now."

Sophia's own stomach grumbled, a sensation that seemed to have left her once the thirst had taken over. But now that she'd had enough to drink, she ached for something to eat. "Me too," she said. "I'll make you a promise. Once we get to town, I'll bake you something."

His smiled lingered a second, and then his brow furrowed, erasing the expression most men would have when a lady offered to cook for him. "You needn't do that. My mother—"

"Is a wonderful cook, I'm certain. But you rescued *me* from those awful bandits, and found us a way back to civilization. I think the least I owe you is a loaf of good bread or a custard pie." She held her breath, hoping he might agree.

Finally, he nodded, although his expression remained tight. "All right, then. I've not yet turned down anything that promises to make my stomach happy."

Sophia bit her lip to keep from smiling as she fished the hot stones from the bowl with the bigger rock to let the water cool. Her mother always said that the best way to win a man over was through good cooking. And while Sophia was perhaps only a moderately decent cook, her baked goods had always drawn compliments. Surely Matthew would think more highly of her then, and if she could also find him a wife . . . well, her work would be done.

But she frowned as she watched the steam rise from the little bowl. Instead of gaining satisfaction from her plans, she just felt . . . empty.

And when she glanced up at Matthew, she knew exactly why.

She didn't wish to find him another wife.

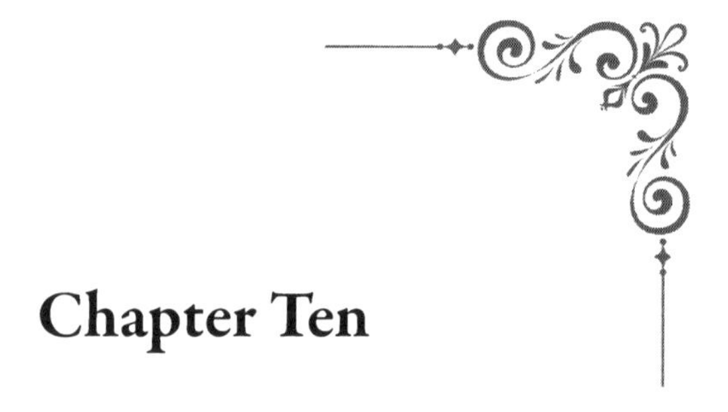

Chapter Ten

THE WALK INTO PUEBLO the following day wasn't very far. And thanks to Miss Zane's money—of which she apparently had given the outlaws only a fraction—they were able to purchase food, a night's stay at a boarding house, and two train tickets to Crest Stone.

Little pangs of guilt carved out a bit of Matthew's soul as he took the seat beside Miss Zane on the train. Not only had she saved them by finding a way to boil that river water, she'd also ensured they had food and had made certain they didn't need to walk to Crest Stone. Matthew was resolved to pay her back once he reached home, despite her protestations.

By some fortunate circumstance, the sheriff's office had held onto Miss Zane's carpetbag. The sheriff wasn't in to hear their account of what had happened, and the deputy waved them off when Matthew offered to tell him. Matthew's own belongings were long gone, tied onto the saddle of the horse that now rode with that band of outlaws, and he had to admit he felt rumpled and out of place accompanying her on the train.

"It is nice to travel while sitting, isn't it?" she asked him, a sweet smile on her scrubbed clean face.

"It is. I'd prefer never to have to traipse through the desert again," he replied.

"Well, you did a fine job of leading us to safety." Her brown eyes sparkled with some unnamed joy as the train jolted into motion.

Matthew resisted the urge to pull at his collar. "I did my best." There was a long pause while Sophia looked out the window at the platform slowly passing by.

"You look very nice today," he said. It was meant to be an off-hand sort of remark, one meant to fill the silence, but it felt awkward coming out of his mouth and Matthew wished he'd commented on the weather instead.

"Thank you." Sophia smoothed her skirt, and he thought he saw a slight flush creep into her cheeks.

It almost made him think she hadn't been complimented very often, although he couldn't fathom why. Miss Zane ought to have had herds of suitors knocking on her door in Kansas City. But something told him that wasn't the case.

How odd that they could have spent all that time walking together, and he still didn't know that much about her.

"I'm afraid both of my dresses are nearly worn through from all those months on the wagon," Miss Zane said, her fingers pulling some at the sprigged fabric. "I hope there is a good dressmaker in Crest Stone."

"There is a small place that's recently opened. I overheard my mother speaking of it."

Miss Zane nodded. "Then I will most certainly pay the shop a visit. I hardly need a wardrobe full of clothing, but a couple of decent dresses that aren't on the verge of springing holes would be nice."

Where had she gotten all of that money? Matthew hadn't realized she'd kept some back from the outlaws, but apparently she had enough that she not only appeared unconcerned about paying for lodging in Crest Stone, she also had plans to purchase new dresses. When he'd told her he would repay her once they reached Crest Stone, she'd said it was a much better use of her money than giving it to the man who had wished to marry her back in Kansas City.

That had certainly caught his attention. When he pressed, she had said no more. But a woman of her means could have set herself up nicely without the need for marriage. What had possessed her to jump onto a wagon train, of all things? And despite her wealth, she hardly seemed *wealthy*, as least as much as Matthew had known people of great means. Which seemed to indicate she wasn't wealthy at all . . . but in that case, where had the money come from?

Something about the situation sat uneasy in his bones. But the worry flitted away the second Miss Zane lifted her eyes to meet his. How could a woman who'd deceived an entire wagon train—and him—to come out here look so very innocent and clear of conscience? And then there were her actions in town. She easily could have taken her leave of him, left him to fend for himself while she took a room and purchased only one train ticket.

But she didn't. And that was only the latest in her long list of good deeds and positive attributes. *Who* was Miss Zane?

"I must admit that I envy the way you speak of your mother—and your father," she said.

Matthew's forehead creased until he remembered that he'd mentioned hearing of the dressmaker from his mother. "They're good people."

"I can see that in their son." Her words settled on him like a warm quilt. "It makes me miss my own parents."

"You'll have to write them once we arrive," he said.

But Miss Zane shook her head. "I wish I could, although if that were possible, I wouldn't be here. They've both passed on, not long before I left home." Her eyes shone with unshed tears and she caught her lip between her teeth.

Her distress pierced Matthew's heart. Without thinking, he laid a hand on her arm. She stiffened, but just for a second, and despite his mind telling him it was too much, too dangerous, and too . . . *everything*, he left his hand where it was.

It felt right, to offer her some degree of comfort like this.

"I'm sorry to hear that. I can't imagine how hard that was for you," he said.

"It was. They were both ill for some time, but that didn't make their passing any easier. They were wonderful parents. I couldn't have asked for any better. I was their only child, and so they doted on me." The sadness that had consumed those beautiful brown eyes seemed to diminish, and she turned just slightly toward him. "Tell me about your parents. Do you have many siblings? Somehow I picture you with a multitude of little sisters."

Matthew laughed. "You would be incorrect, Miss Zane."

"Sophia, please. After all, I feel we've gotten to know each other rather well over the past few days." Her smile was utterly disarming, and any pretense of formality Matthew tried to keep in place shattered immediately.

It wouldn't hurt to call her by her given name. After all, she'd already indicated a desire to help him find a wife. And he knew better than to pursue anything with a woman who

. . . Matthew's thoughts careened to a halt. He kept thinking of her as a deceiver, as a woman who would say anything to get what she needed. But there was so much more to Miss Zane—Sophia—than he'd first thought.

And even more that he'd like to learn about her.

"All right, Sophia it is. And no, I have no little sisters. Or brothers, for that matter. I'm also my parents' only child," he said.

"How interesting." She studied him intently, as if she were searching for something, and Matthew became acutely aware that his hand still rested on her arm. He slowly pulled it away, and Sophia tilted her head.

"What is interesting?"

"You know, I've heard people say that children with no siblings grow up to be selfish and demanding. But you appear to be neither."

"I could say the same for you," he replied.

"I was selfish when I joined the wagon train using Miss Timperman's name." Sophia ducked her head. "I am truly sorry for pretending to be her."

While he'd wished he'd known who she was from the start . . . Had it hurt anything, really? Aside from his heart, which would have been bruised when the wagons arrived without Miss Timperman anyway.

"It's in the past," he said. "I hold no grudge against you."

Her smile seemed to fill the entire car with sunshine. "Thank you. You don't know how much your forgiveness means to me. I would like to repay you for the fee you must have provided Miss Timperman for the wagon journey."

Matthew waved a hand. "Please don't, especially after all you've done. I'm only glad it went to help you arrive, instead of in her pocket."

Sophia chewed her lip a moment. "She must have changed her mind at the last minute, if she'd already paid for the journey."

He nodded. "I suppose that's a mystery I'll never solve."

"Well, for what it's worth, I'm happy to be here. Oh, look! The mountains have grown larger!" She pointed out the window, her eyes wide with delight.

And Matthew couldn't keep the smile off his face. Sophia's contagious joy pushed the depressing thought of Miss Timperman's rejection right out of his head.

This, he decided, would be the most enjoyable train journey he'd ever undertaken.

Chapter Eleven

BY THE TIME THE TRAIN arrived in Crest Stone, Sophia was certain she'd never seen any place so beautiful. The town sat nestled in a little valley flanked by two mountain ranges, one low and dark off to the east and the other closer and snow-capped immediately to the west. It felt like something out of a storybook as the train rolled through the valley filled with wildflowers, birds, and deer that went scampering the moment the train drew too close.

She laid a hand on her hat when she stepped onto the platform to keep the breeze from lifting it and sending it sailing. Matthew had her bag and had offered to walk her to the boarding house at the edge of town. Not that the edge of town was all that far off. Sophia could see both ends from where they stood just in front of the depot.

"It isn't very far from here," Matthew said unnecessarily as they began to stroll down the plank sidewalk. "You'll like the Darbys. They're a brother and sister who came here the same time we did, last year. They run a nice, reputable establishment."

That was reassuring, considering some of the men they passed looked rougher than even the toughest men Sophia had seen back in Kansas City. "Is it . . . is it safe here?" she asked as they passed a saloon that appeared rowdier than any place should be during the daylight hours.

Matthew laughed, and when she shot him an irritated look, he tried to stop. "I'm sorry," he said. "It's just that you've survived a wagon journey of hundreds and hundreds of miles, kidnapping by bandits, and a trek through the desert with very little water. You're stronger than nearly any man you'll meet in this town."

Sophia pressed her lips together as she tried not to grin. He was right. With everything she had been through, if any man dared to approach her with any less than respectable manner, she'd probably smack him without a second thought.

"It's safe enough, though. I wouldn't advise wandering about after dark, but we have a good marshal who keeps things in line." Matthew stopped in front of one of the last buildings before the town gave way to wilderness.

Sophia glanced up at the nondescript building. *Darby's Boarding House* was painted simply and unpretentiously on a sign above the door. She followed Matthew inside where he arranged for a room for her.

"Why don't I come back at six o'clock? You can have dinner with us," he said while Mr. Darby searched for a key.

"I would love that." Having a meal with someone she already knew was infinitely preferable to eating with strangers at the boarding house.

Matthew bid her farewell, and Sophia spent the afternoon unpacking the small amount of items she'd brought with her, resting, and washing her remaining clothing. A friendly woman named Abigail helped her work on removing a stain from her skirt, and told Sophia about her burgeoning laundry business.

"There isn't anyone else in town taking in laundry. I'm the first, and I'll be able to do even more once I rent out a storefront," she said. "I've been saving for months."

Sophia nodded, unable to put her awe into words. Why, she'd never even thought of starting her own business. How many more opportunities existed here that had never crossed her mind?

She freshened up as best she could in the well-worn dress she'd worn on the train, and by the time Matthew arrived, she was downstairs, ready and waiting.

He smiled the moment he saw her, and Sophia's face went warm. Just a look from him sent her mind into a flurry and her cheeks flaming, and it was something she had to figure out how to control. He had no interest in her. He'd wanted Miss Timperman—or someone like her. A demure sort who would never think of pretending to be someone she was not. The best thing Sophia could do for Matthew was to help him find a new bride, and in doing so, perhaps she'd earn his respect.

You've already done that, a little voice in the back of her mind said as they walked along the sidewalk and he offered her his arm. She took it and let herself revel in the protective feel of the gesture. If he didn't have at least some degree of respect and concern for her, he certainly wouldn't have invited her for a meal with his parents, much less offered an arm to escort her to his home.

Matthew spoke on easy topics as they strode down the street—which businesses were new, who was in charge of what, what the hotel on the hill looked like inside, and how lovely the little church in town was. They stopped just past that church, at a small home next door.

"My father is especially happy with how the church has grown. I think he despaired of having very few congregants when we first arrived here," Matthew said, his eyes on the church.

Sophia looked from the house to the church and back again as the pieces of the puzzle fit together. "Your father is the pastor?" She asked the question even though she thought she already knew the answer.

"Yes. I promise he's the cheerful sort, and not the kind prone to fire and brimstone," Matthew said with a crooked grin.

Sophia laughed. "Well, that would have been fine too. I'm sorry, I think I had pictured your parents on a farm or . . . or . . ." She trailed off, not entirely certain what she *had* expected. But certainly not among the most important people in town.

"It could have been worse," Matthew said as he opened the door to the house. "He could have been mayor."

That made Sophia laugh again, and she was grateful not to have to meet a mayor in her threadbare trail dress. She followed Matthew inside the small but comfortable-looking home.

"Hello, I'm here!" he cried in a way so familiar it made Sophia's heart clench. Hadn't she walked into her own home in Kansas City and said those exact same words hundreds of times? The house itself reminded her of home, too, with its simple layout and scent of something baking.

"Neither of them were home earlier," he said to Sophia as he led her into a cramped but light-filled dining room. "Why don't you wait here while I find them?"

"They don't know I'm here?" Sophia rested her hands on the back of a chair. "Perhaps I should come another day—"

"Of course not." Matthew paused by the door. "My parents would never turn away a guest. Besides, Mama always makes enough for half the town. We have guests more nights than not." He gave her a wink before disappearing down the hallway.

Sophia barely had time to compose her thoughts before he returned with a smaller, rounder, female version of himself. Sophia instantly liked Mrs. Canton with her pink cheeks, kind smile, and hair that refused to stay put in its pins.

Mrs. Canton wiped her hands on a cloth she held. "You must be Miss Zane. What a pleasure to meet you!"

No one had ever sounded as enthused to meet Sophia before. She smiled back at Mrs. Canton. "It is wonderful to meet you too. I hope I'm not intruding—"

"Nonsense." Mrs. Canton waved her hand in the exact same way Matthew had done when they were on the train. "All are welcome here. We have plenty!"

"Thank you," Sophia said warmly. "May I help in some way? It's the least I could do considering Mat—Mr. Canton saved my life."

Her slip of the tongue hadn't gone unnoticed, as Mrs. Canton's eyebrows quirked up when she nearly called Matthew by his given name. But thankfully, Mrs. Canton seemed far more interested in the last bit of information.

"That sounds like quite a tale." She leaned in, as eager as a child to hear it.

"We can spin the entire story over dinner, but suffice to say that a band of outlaws kidnapped Miss Zane, and I—thinking she was Miss Timperman—went after her. They took nearly everything we had, but we walked back to safety in Pueblo after a few days' journey." Matthew glanced at Sophia, and with just a look, she was instantly back in the desert with him, wondering if they would survive.

They shared a smile until Mrs. Canton spoke. "That does sound like an incredible story." But something had gone missing from her voice, and the smile she gave felt forced. "Miss Zane, why don't you make yourself at home here? Matthew, I'll need your help."

Matthew had noticed the change in her demeanor too, his mouth settling into a straight line as he nodded. But he turned and gave Sophia a reassuring nod before leaving, and she sank into one of the dining room chairs.

Had she done something that had made Mrs. Canton wary of her? Matthew hadn't conveyed her deception—he'd simply said that he'd assumed she was Miss Timperman—so that couldn't be it. Was it something in her own demeanor?

Sophia glanced down at her dress, as if that would give her the answer. She appeared perfectly normal—worn but clean dress and shoes, gloves, hat, tidy hair. She picked up a spoon and peered at her reflection. Nothing seemed amiss. Besides, even if her nose was covered in boils and her dress was hardly presentable, she doubted Mrs. Canton would turn her away. She was a godly woman, after all.

No, it had to be something in the brief story Matthew had told her.

But what?

Chapter Twelve

SOPHIA WAS QUIET DURING the walk back to the boarding house. After filling up far too much of the conversation himself, Matthew finally asked if something was on her mind.

She worried her lip as he steered her across the road from the saloon. There were far too many men gathered out front at this hour, and the last thing he felt like doing was trying to escort a lady through that crowd.

"I fear I did something to upset your mother," she finally said when they reached the sidewalk on the opposite side of the road. She stopped and glanced down at her shoes. Thankfully, the street was dry enough that not much had stuck to them.

Her actions gave Matthew time to think. She was right in noticing that something felt strained. And he knew exactly why. "You didn't. It was . . ." He trailed off, trying to figure out the best way to relay his mother's concerns. "She worried about the time we spent alone together."

Sophia looked up from her shoes and blinked at him. The darkness hid any hint of red that might have come to her cheeks.

"I told her there was nothing to be concerned about. Our minds were entirely on water and getting to Pueblo."

She nodded. "And my deception," she added softly, and Matthew chuckled.

"Yes, that too." He waited for her to take his arm before they continued. "I thought I'd alleviated her concerns, but perhaps she needs more time."

"I did like them both very much," Sophia said as she stepped around a stack of empty crates that had been left in front of a shop. "Your mother is very kind, and your father made me laugh."

Matthew smiled. "His sense of humor is well known throughout town. Sometimes I think half the congregation comes for his jokes rather than his preaching—but don't tell him that."

"I promise to keep it to myself." Sophia said, amusement in her voice as they crossed the less worn road—and the railroad tracks in the middle of it—at the end of town to reach the boarding house.

"Would you like me to show you around town tomorrow? Perhaps I can get a carriage and we can drive down to the creek and out into the valley." He bit off the end of the words abruptly, realizing his offer sounded more like something one might do for a lady he wanted to court rather than . . . What would he call Sophia? A friend? That didn't feel right, after all they'd survived. And yet the thought of anyone else coming to take her for a similar drive made his blood run hot.

"Only if you promise to bring plenty of water," she said, the corner of her mouth curved up into a teasing grin.

Matthew laughed. "I promise." He didn't mention that he'd have to pay the livery for the horses he'd lost first. He ought to be concerned about losing the money he was so carefully saving to build on the land he'd purchased, but it was hard to worry about such things when Sophia looked at him with a joyful expectancy in her eyes.

"I'll come after I finish at my office tomorrow," he said.

She nodded as she pressed the door open. "Perhaps we'll discover a place where I might ask for work."

She didn't seem too concerned about running low on the money she had. Matthew wasn't certain how much there was, but if it was plentiful, he couldn't help but admire her desire to spend as little of it as possible. "I can ask around, if you'd like."

The smile she gave him then almost had him offering his own job to her. "That would be very kind. Thank you, Matthew."

She disappeared inside, and he stood there a moment like a man lost, the sound of her voice around his name replaying in his head. He wondered if anyone had ever told her how melodic her voice was. He'd never heard his own name spoken with such care.

He stepped away from the boarding house and the absurdity of his own thoughts seemed to hit him in his face. He was supposed to be wary of her, this woman who'd pretended to be his fiancée.

And yet he wasn't. She'd proven over and again that she was more than the deception . . . and perhaps it was time he accepted her for everything she'd shown him she was since then.

As soon as that thought crossed his mind, Matthew's soul felt ten times lighter. Yes, he was still hurt that Miss Timperman hadn't come, but even that seemed as if it might have been for the best now. The night around him felt less dark, and the shouts coming from the saloon sounded joyful rather than threatening.

The world itself felt so much more promising—until he stepped through the door of his parents' home.

Both Mama and Father sat in the parlor, which wasn't unusual for this hour. But it was the fact that Mama held neither sewing nor a book, and Father sat perfectly straight in his chair rather than in his normal relaxed posture, that indicated something was wrong.

Matthew paused just inside the door, not entirely certain he wanted to sit down amid the tension in the air. He mentally ran through anything that could have caused a disruption in his parents' usual evening routine. Someone was sick—no, Father would be at their home, comforting them. Death—no, again, Father would be with the family and Mama would be cooking up a storm in the kitchen as if food somehow eased grief. Bad news from family back in Illinois—that was a possibility.

"Please sit, son," Father said, and in that moment Matthew knew this was about him.

He perched on the edge of the settee across from them. How many times had guests sat here, enjoying Mama's stories and Father's jokes, or seeking counsel late into the night from Father. Now he was the one sitting here, and he was sure it wasn't jokes or stories he'd be getting. "Is this about Miss Zane?" It was best to just get it out there rather than waiting for the inevitable.

"It is," Mama said. "I relayed my concerns to your father, and we're in agreement."

Matthew's eyebrows knitted together. "I told you we merely tried to survive. Our concerns were water and safety, and that was all. Besides, I had just learned Miss Timperman wasn't coming."

His parents looked at each other.

"Surely you believe me?" He was hardly a boy, testing their patience with lies. And although as a grown man, he didn't need their permission or guidance to do anything, he wanted their respect.

"We believe you, son," Father said. "You're a good man, and we're comforted by that each and every day. But this isn't about what did or didn't happen."

Matthew's heart fell as he realized what his father meant.

"As people in town start to hear your story—and they will, if you wish to be truthful—they'll make assumptions," Mama said, her voice as gentle as it had always been.

"Assumptions that won't reflect well on Miss Zane," Father added.

Matthew dug his fingers into the edge of the settee. Just the thought of anyone casting aspersions on Sophia's reputation made him want to hit something, and he wasn't the sort of man who went looking for fights. "I won't let that happen," he said in a low voice.

"I'm afraid you won't have control over whether it does or doesn't happen," Father said.

"They'll talk anyway." Mama folded her hands in her lap. "Are you going to be in every parlor in town? At every store counter and every table in the diner and the hotel?"

Matthew swallowed as he realized they were right. If people talked, he could do nothing about it. Nothing at all unless they approached him or Sophia directly. And in the meantime, the gossip . . . He closed his eyes for a second, desperately seeking a way to keep it all from happening. "We won't tell anyone."

Mama shook her head, and Father's expression radiated empathy.

"Think of how that will make you feel. How it will make her feel, if you have to keep such a difficult experience to yourselves. To never tell a soul. What will happen if the sheriff needs information on those outlaws? Will you opt to let them continue terrorizing people? What if Miss Zane finds a young man to marry? Is she supposed to never tell him about what happened?" Father's voice was even and kind, the way it was when he wanted people to truly think about a situation.

Matthew sighed. He was right. There were far too many things that could go wrong if they never told anyone about Sophia's kidnapping and their subsequent journey through the desert. "Then what do I do?"

Father looked to Mama, who pressed her lips together as if she were gathering her courage. Matthew's hands dug farther into the settee.

"While you walked Miss Zane home, your father and I discussed it. And the only conclusion we could come to was that you ought to marry Miss Zane."

Chapter Thirteen

IT WAS A LITTLE AFTER three o'clock the next day when Matthew sent a note to the boarding house to let Sophia know he would be arriving with a carriage in just over an hour. When he arrived, she eagerly followed him outside to see a carriage with two horses just out front.

"It's lovely!" She clasped her hands together in delight. "I haven't ridden in a carriage in so long. My father used to rent one on occasion, and I just loved it."

Matthew smiled as he extended a hand to assist her with climbing inside. "I can't say I've driven one recently. It'll be a nice change."

Sophia took his hand. Even through her glove, she could feel the warmth of his fingers clasping hers. It was enough to make her entire body grow uncomfortably hot, and she couldn't decide if she was relieved or disappointed when she settled herself in the carriage and he let go.

The little carriage swayed as Matthew climbed inside. Sophia gripped the edges of the seat as the carriage lurched into motion. The horses moved at a slow pace down the road.

"How is the little restaurant there?" Sophia asked as they passed the eatery.

"It's good. It doesn't measure up to home cooking, of course, but the proprietor is a nice enough fellow." Matthew kept his eyes on the horses as he spoke.

Sophia turned her head to watch the diner disappear behind them. "Do you suppose he might need some help? I could cook, or serve the customers."

"Perhaps," Matthew said. Sophia waited for him to elaborate, but he didn't. "There's the mercantile." He nodded toward a building across the road. "The owner and his wife arrived here when this place was nothing but a few abandoned buildings."

"Did they intend to farm?" Sophia couldn't imagine why else someone would come to a town that didn't yet exist to start a mercantile.

Matthew shook his head as he steered the horses around a wagon stopped outside the mercantile. "Drexel was hired on to build the hotel up on the hill, and Mrs. Drexel was one of the first ladies who arrived to work there."

Sophia's eyes found the hotel—easy to spot since it stood higher than anything else in town. It was a grand looking place for such a tiny town. "Do you suppose the hotel might hire me on? They have a restaurant, don't they?"

"It comes with a contract that prohibits courting." Matthew stated this fact as if Sophia had a plethora of men falling over themselves to pay her visits.

She was about to ask more about the hotel when another opportunity appeared closer to their carriage. "Oh! What about the post office? Or the telegraph service? Might they want assistance?"

Matthew clucked to the horses before shaking his head yet again. "An older fellow is the town postmaster and telegraph operator. He employs a young boy as an assistant. If he'd wanted someone else, I imagine he would have hired another man on by now."

Sophia bit down on her lip. It seemed as if Matthew didn't want her to find work at all. "Well, could you kindly suggest somewhere that might need help? I'm not particular." Her voice had more of an edge to it than she wanted, but it certainly *was* frustrating that he wasn't being more encouraging.

He sighed as he directed the horses to stop for a couple of men crossing the road. And then he finally looked at her, his expression serious. "I'm sorry. I have something I must speak to you about, and this isn't the place. May I take us somewhere more private?"

For the life of her, Sophia couldn't imagine what he wished to speak of that couldn't be talked about right here. But she nodded anyway. "That would be fine. Where should we go?"

He gave her a little smile. "I have the perfect place." He urged the horses into a walk again, and before long, they'd reached the edge of town. The carriage followed the road north, alongside the railroad tracks that bisected the town.

They didn't speak—Sophia didn't know what to say now that Matthew had conveyed the need to talk about something important. So she spent the ride admiring the scenery and pondering the possibilities.

It must be about his search for a wife. It would make sense that he wouldn't wish to talk about that within earshot of the town's residents. Who knew who might overhear and gossip about the poor man whose intended had changed her mind?

About twenty minutes outside of town, Matthew turned to the east, off the road and into the grasses and sage near the rise of a small hill. He headed toward the dark mountains—the Wet Mountains, Sophia recalled from dinner the night before. The ones after which this valley, the Wet Mountain Valley, was named. She had to crane her neck around the edge of the carriage to see the snowcapped Sangre de Cristo range behind them.

Just as she was about to ask Matthew where they were headed, he stopped the carriage near a stand of pines. Sophia looked around her, unable to puzzle out why he'd stopped here. He leapt out of the carriage and came around to her side to help her out. When she was safely on the ground, he secured the horses while she walked past the carriage to admire the landscape.

It wasn't much different here from in town, save for the lack of buildings, of course. And they were a bit farther away from the bigger mountains to the west. There was the echo of a gurgling stream somewhere nearby, and here and there, little hills punctuated the mostly flat terrain. A bird sang from one of the pine trees, and a smile tugged its way onto Sophia's face.

This was, she decided, the most peaceful place she'd even seen.

"Wouldn't this be a lovely spot to build a home?" she asked Matthew when he joined her. She could almost picture it, a little wooden house with a wide, welcoming porch, a chicken coop in the rear, and a line to dry laundry. "Right there." She pointed at the perfect spot. "Perhaps with a stable for horses right there. And of course a couple of comfortable chairs on the front porch."

When he said nothing, she glanced up at him to find him watching her with the most serene expression on his face.

"What is it?" she asked. "Do you love chairs on a porch as much as I do?"

"No," he said, shaking his head. "I mean, yes, I do, but that isn't it." He drew in a breath and looked over the land toward the east. "This is my land."

Sophia's eyes widened at the thought of owning such a place. "I . . . I . . ." She couldn't put her thoughts into words. "You are very lucky," she finally managed to say, though the words were hardly enough to convey her amazement.

"I am," he said, his voice quiet. "To have found no one had purchased this already, anyway. I worked for years to save the money to buy my own property, first in Montana, and more recently here. When I was going through the records in the land office, I discovered this parcel. And when I rode out here to see it, I knew it was exactly what I'd been waiting for."

"It's perfect," Sophia said, her eyes drinking in the rise and fall of the little hills, the silver of the sage, the way the blue sky met the tops of the shadowed mountains.

"I plan to build a ranch here. It's an ideal place. Close enough to the railroad, but with its own water source. Near enough to town for necessities, but far enough away to give the cattle room to graze."

Sophia nodded as he spoke. She didn't know the first thing about ranching, but listening to him talk about it, she wanted to know more.

She furrowed her brow as he discussed how he planned to slowly build the ranch. Was this why he'd brought her here? To explain his dreams? Perhaps he wanted her to see the place in order to better convey his plans to the ladies who wrote to him. Did that mean he wished her to write the letters, then?

She hadn't intended to do that, and her stomach twisted in a strange way at the thought of trying to convince some stranger to agree to marry this good-hearted, kind man.

"Sophia?" His voice broke into her thoughts as the bird in the pines took flight, feathered wings flying so close that Sophia thought she could reach out and touch their softness with her fingers. "Are you all right?"

"Yes, I am. But Matthew . . . Why did you bring me here?" It was best to get to the point immediately. If he wished her to be the letter writer, she'd need to learn more about what precisely he hoped to find in a wife. Even if the idea left her feeling as if she were smothering.

He drew in a deep breath, his chest expanding—and oh, heavens—why was she looking at his chest? Sophia forced her eyes to his face, but that wasn't much easier, because all she could think then was that some woman from Wisconsin or Connecticut or wherever wouldn't *truly* appreciate how the deep blue of his eyes looked like the Colorado sky at twilight.

He turned to her then, took another deep breath, and then said, "I brought you here to ask you to marry me."

Chapter Fourteen

THE SECONDS AFTER HE asked the question seemed to stretch on for a day. Matthew began to think that Sophia hadn't heard him when she finally spoke up.

"I can't do that," she said softly.

He swallowed as despair rose up his throat. This was awkward enough, asking a woman he'd only known for days to marry him, but now she was turning him down, and—

No. She couldn't turn him down. He hadn't yet explained himself. Matthew pushed down the utter disappointment he hadn't expected at all.

"Please, hear me out." He reached for her hand, and she let him take it. It felt so natural, cradling her smaller hand within his. He forced his mind away from that thought to what he needed to say. "This is for the best. And I confess I was remiss in not thinking about the repercussions myself. My parents were the ones who brought it up, and I fear they're right."

"Repercussions?" she repeated, her eyebrows furrowing.

"To our journey across the desert together." He waited a moment to see if she understood.

And she did, judging by the way her lips formed a small "o" and her eyes widened. "But you told them nothing happened . . ."

He nodded. "Of course I did. And they don't doubt me. But what they fear is that as our story makes it way out and travels through town, others might think differently."

"I told a couple of the girls about it all today, over the noon meal," she said in a quiet voice. Then she closed her eyes. When she opened them, it was as if recognition had dawned. "I heard them whispering when I left, but I didn't think anything of it at the time."

"My parents fear for your reputation. And to be honest, Sophia, so do I." That hardly conveyed the white hot anger that singed his insides whenever he thought of someone saying something untoward about Sophia.

She looked away, off toward where the town sat, miles from here. "But you don't want to marry me."

Her words sliced into his heart. And right then, he knew with absolute certainty, that she was wrong.

He *did* want to marry her.

Swallowing to press back the emotion that welled up in his throat, Matthew took a moment before he spoke. "You're incorrect. I would very much like you to be my wife."

Her eyes found his then, and she tilted her head as if she were trying to suss out the truth. "I fear you're only saying that out of duty. You wanted a wife like Miss Timperman, and I was going to help you find one."

Matthew shook his head. "I didn't *know* Miss Timperman, aside from what she told me in letters. And when it came time, she changed her mind without a word to me. So, no, I don't want Miss Timperman."

Sophia took a step toward him, those brown eyes searching his and gently prying her hand from his own. "Then what *do* you want?"

His breath hitched in his throat. *You*. But the word stuck there like the pit from a cherry. "I . . . I want someone courageous. Joyful. Unafraid of challenges or hard times. Kind and caring. Smart. Generous. Honest." He paused, looking for some sign in her expression that showed she was changing her mind.

"I believe you want a woman who doesn't truly exist. No one is that perfect, Matthew." Her voice skittered across him like a leaf on the wind.

He shook his head, rubbing his temple. "That isn't what I meant. I know that. What I was trying to say was that I believe you fit all of those qualities—most of the time." He added a little smile, hoping to lighten the moment.

She smiled too, but it was fleeting. "This isn't necessary. I could take the train to another town. Go where no one knows me or what happened."

"Do you wish to keep that journey we took a secret forever?" He paused. "And do you wish to be alone? Here, you have me and my family, the girls you've met at the boarding house. I can introduce you to other ladies at the church."

Sophia's lips pushed together again, and he knew he was getting somewhere. The breeze kicked the little strands of hair around her face into a dance, and she pushed them away impatiently. "I hadn't planned to marry immediately."

It sounded as if she wanted to say more, so he waited. But when she didn't speak again, he realized what might be bothering her. "I understand. Please know I'm not the sort of man to push anything on you that you aren't ready for. We can pretend as if this is the mail-order arrangement I'd counted on."

Her cheeks went a pleasing shade of pink. He was so close to having her say yes.

"And while I may not be the handsomest man around, I imagine I'm a sight better looking than that fellow who was pestering you in Kansas City."

That did it. Her reticence gave way, and she laughed, the joy he'd come to love seeing upon her face back again.

"You are that, indeed," she said, her voice breathy from the laughter. She turned then, her eyes tracing the land, from the rise of the hills in the distance to the mountains far to the east to the graceful line of the grasses leading the way south before she found him again. "Would we live here?"

His heart warmed at her obvious appreciation for this land he loved so much. "Yes, as soon as I could get a house built. In the meantime, my parents have room—unless you'd prefer to take up a room in the hotel—"

Sophia shook her head. "No, it would take so much longer to accumulate the funds needed to build if we did that."

And again he marveled at her practicality. Not many women would have been willing to live in such an arrangement. "Does this mean you're saying yes?"

Her lips curved into a smile. "Yes. I'm saying yes."

Matthew let out a shout and threw his arms around her waist. He lifted her just barely off the ground and swung her around. Sophia laughed, and when he set her down, he let his hands remain in place on her waist.

She looked up at him with a hesitant reverence. As if she still wasn't entirely certain about this marriage.

And right then and there, Matthew vowed he'd prove to her that she wouldn't regret it.

Chapter Fifteen

THE NEXT FEW DAYS WERE a whirlwind. The girls at the boardinghouse cooed with glee when Sophia told them of her upcoming nuptials. One of them—a shy girl from some city back East—offered to lend Sophia her finest dress for the occasion. It was a shimmering silk concoction, somewhere between the shade of pearl and champagne, and Sophia could imagine it swirling about a dance floor in New York or Boston.

She gratefully accepted. The two dresses she had ordered from the dressmaker wouldn't be finished for a while, and showing up to one's wedding in a dress that had been through a wagon journey, a kidnapping, and a long walk to civilization felt far too casual.

And then, before she knew it, Sophia was standing in Crest Stone's only church, with Reverend Canton presiding and Matthew holding both of her hands in his. Mrs. Canton played the organ, while the girls from the boarding house and Matthew's friends from town filled the pews.

For a moment, a wild feeling of regret raced through her. What was she doing? She hardly knew Matthew! He seemed to have decided she was trustworthy—thank goodness—but then there was the small matter of the money she'd inherited. He knew nothing of Mr. Durham's claim on it.

His eyes caught hers in that moment, and her mind stopped instantly. He gave her a slight smile as his father talked about cherishing one another—and then it all felt right.

Her trip West had turned out this way for a reason. And perhaps she ought to trust in that. Once married to Matthew, she'd be safe from gossip. She would tell him about the money. What did it matter anyway if Mr. Durham thought it was his? He was in Kansas City, hundreds and hundreds of miles away, without a clue where she had gone.

She was safe here. She was safe with Matthew.

When Reverend Canton pronounced them husband and wife, Matthew's hands tightened around hers. He leaned forward, and ever so gently, pressed his lips to hers. Sophia's eyes fluttered shut, and everything around her fell away except for him. How could such a simple, gentle touch be filled with so much promise?

Sophia didn't know, but she did know one thing—she never wanted it to end. Instead, she wanted to press herself closer to him, make him wrap his arms around her as he did when he proposed marriage by the pine trees on his land. But all too soon, it was over. He pulled away, and she opened her eyes, blinking away the light and the presence of so many people.

"Congratulations," Reverend Canton said. He wrapped his son into a hug, and Sophia stepped back, marveling at the connection the two shared. It reminded her of her own family, and her heart simultaneously ached and leapt with joy over finding another family that was so much like her own.

"The girls from the boarding house brought your bag over," Mrs. Canton said, appearing at Sophia's elbow.

It was a wonderfully kind gesture, saving her from a walk back to the Darbys'. And as Sophia greeted each of the girls, she marveled at how she'd already come to make so many friends. Why, she had more friends here than she'd had when she left Kansas City, and she'd lived there her entire life.

Just as she caught her breath after talking with Mrs. Darby, Matthew brought her to meet friends of his. Her head whirled, trying to remember names. There were the Drexels, who Matthew had mentioned before, his boss Mr. Gilbert from the land office and his wife, Dora, a congenial couple whose last name was Hartley, Mr. and Mrs. McFarland who managed the hotel, a fellow who owned the livery and his lively, friendly wife, the town blacksmith, the banker whose wife had recently given birth to a baby, and so many more. Sophia feared she would never remember all their names.

Finally, the church had emptied, and all that remained were Sophia and Matthew. Even his parents had slipped out.

Exhaustion setting in, Sophia sank to the nearest pew. Matthew sat next to her and she looked up at him, her husband. It was such a strange thing to think about.

"My parents gave us a gift." Matthew shifted as if the gift somehow made him uncomfortable.

"Oh?"

"They want to pay for us to stay at the hotel for a night." He glanced at her as he pulled on his collar. "We don't have to. I know it's—"

A smile curved Sophia's lips. "I think it sounds wonderful."

"You do?"

She nodded. "After all it will be the same sort of situation when we come back to their home, won't it?"

"I suppose." He slapped his hands on his knees. "Well, I guess it's settled. Shall we head there now?"

Sophia stood and took the arm he offered. Together, after collecting what they needed, they made their way down the road and then up the hill toward the imposing hotel. It was hard not to gasp in awe as they grew closer. How had such a place come to be built in Crest Stone? Why, there was even a fountain out front of the hotel's entrance.

"It is awfully magnificent," she said when they reached the doors.

He gave her a smile. "Just wait until you see inside."

And he wasn't wrong. If Sophia had been in awe of the outside, that didn't hold a candle to what she felt stepping into the hotel lobby. Magnificent fireplaces stood on each side of the wide room, a large desk sat straight ahead, and comfortable seating was set in conversational angles here and there. A staircase was positioned off to the right, and the hotel branched out with long wings on either side of the desk.

She was glad Matthew was here because she couldn't have found her voice. He approached the desk and told the clerk that they had a room waiting.

In no time at all, the clerk had handed Matthew a key, and had asked him to sign his name in a large ledger book. That done, they stepped away from the desk.

Their room was upstairs, a nicely furnished space on the second floor, and Sophia particularly loved the view out the window toward the northeast. She could just make out the wet mountains off in the distance, and she wondered if she could see Matthew's land from here.

"It's that direction," he said.

She turned and immediately bumped his chest with her shoulder. "I'm sorry." She went to take a step back only to find there wasn't enough space for that.

"It's quite all right. I don't think I'm permanently injured." He gave her a lilting smile but didn't move away.

His proximity made her swallow. "How did you know I was looking for the land?"

"Because I was looking for the same thing." He held her gaze for a moment and just as Sophia thought she might burst from the tension, he said, "Dinner isn't served until six o'clock. We have some time. Would you like to go down and see the creek?"

She nodded without necessarily thinking about what she was agreeing to. It was hard to think at all with him standing this close to her.

They left after Sophia changed into a different dress. The creek sat behind the hotel, hidden away by trees. Sophia gasped when she first saw it. The lazy water ran clear and cool over rocks. The tall snowy mountains began to climb directly behind it. It was like their own private place, with no one else around behind these trees.

"It's called Silver Creek." Matthew stood on the bank, his hands clasped behind him.

"I love it." Sophia turned and smiled at him. "It's the most beautiful setting, with the mountains and the trees," she said as her eyes feasted on the scenery again.

"Would you like to sit?" Matthew gestured at a large flat stone nearby.

Sophia scurried over and took a seat on the edge of the stone. He sank down next to her, and for a few minutes, they sat in silence, enjoying the sounds of the water and the wind through the trees.

"I never knew such a place existed." How could she ever have dreamed of something that looked like this back in Kansas City?

"It is incredible," Matthew said as he stretched out his legs in front of him. "My dad likes to call it God's artwork."

"That's an apt description." Sophia drew in the cool pine scented air as she remembered all that had happened that day. "The wedding was lovely." She turned to look at Matthew. "Thank you."

"I'm glad I could give you that," he said. "I hope I can give you everything you need."

Sophia's stomach churned at his words. He was so genuine and kind, and yet she hadn't even told him about the money.

Her concern must've shown on her face. Matthew's eyebrows knitted together. She dug her fingers into the rock. Now was just as good a time as any. She couldn't go on keeping the secret. He opened his mouth to say something, but she spoke up first.

"I must tell you about the money. And I hope you won't be angry with me."

Chapter Sixteen

MATTHEW'S HEARTBEAT quickened. A million different possibilities for how she had acquired that large sum flitted through his mind. He stopped those thoughts in their tracks. He trusted Sophia—else he wouldn't have married her.

"I am curious," he finally admitted.

"I imagine so." She gave him a little smile. "It isn't every day you meet a woman carrying so much money in her dress."

Matthew's spirits lifted. It couldn't be too terrible, with the way she was able to make a joke about it. And so he leaned back on his hands and waited.

"It was my parents' money. Specifically, it's money my father earned from his accounting business and invested into other businesses and companies in Kansas City. Growing up, I always wondered why we never had as much as other families in similar lines of work. My mother did all the cleaning and cooking, my father always hired out for a carriage if we needed one, I only got new dresses when I had to have them—that sort of thing. But when I grew older, I learned why." The ghost of a smile lifted her lips, and Matthew fought to keep from reaching up to touch her face.

"He was planning for the future," he said, more to distract himself from his thoughts than to help Sophia tell her story.

She nodded. "You remind me of him in that way."

His insides warmed at the compliment.

"When my parents died, the funds and investments passed to me. I had just met with the attorney and bank to have everything situated when Francis Durham came to my door."

Matthew lifted his eyebrows. "The man who wanted to marry you?"

"Yes." Her face twisted in clear disdain. "But it wasn't an offer made out of any sort of love or kindness. He wanted the money."

Matthew sat up. "That's why you left?"

"It is." Sophia looked down at her hands, which were twisted together in her lap. "At first, he tried to claim the funds were his. That Papa had borrowed the money. And when my attorney asked him for proof, he changed his story and said that he'd given Papa half of each investment. There was, of course, no proof of that either. That's when he insisted I marry him. And when I declined, he . . ."

A simmering fire burst into life deep down inside of Matthew. "He did what?"

Sophia swallowed visibly. "He told me I had no choice. That I would either agree to marry him or he'd find a way to get the money from me, legally or not."

Matthew dug his fingernails into his palms. "Did he do anything?"

"I didn't give him the chance. I went the very next day, withdrew all of the money from the bank, sold as many of the investments as I could, and went to the only place I thought he wouldn't find me—Independence."

"And the wagon train," Matthew finished. "Did you tell anyone where you were going?"

Sophia shook her head. "I didn't have many friends to leave behind, and no family to tell."

A heavy weight lifted from Matthew's shoulders. "That's good."

But Sophia still looked troubled. "I still think about him from time to time. How many young women on their own come through Independence? If he gets the idea that I might have traveled west—" She stopped abruptly and shivered.

Matthew wrapped an arm around her, and it felt as natural as if they'd known each other their entire lives, as if they'd had a long engagement and knew every detail about one another. "You're safe here, I promise you. Even if he were to think you left on a wagon, he'd have to learn that you took on another name. And still, that would lead him as far as Pueblo, where—if that sheriff had time to speak with him—he'd learn you'd been kidnapped. I doubt that deputy bothered to relay the fact that you'd been found. And then what?"

"I don't know." She relaxed a little into his embrace. His breath hitched in his throat at her trust in him.

"Nothing. Nothing will happen."

She turned in his arms. "You can't promise that."

Matthew thought for a moment. "No, I can't. But I can promise you that it is very unlikely, and in the very unlikely chance it does happen, I'll be here to keep you safe."

The sweet smile she gave him was everything. It lit up his soul, and he thought he'd do and say anything to see it again and again.

"I believe you," she said.

And this time he didn't resist. He lifted his free hand and traced the line of her jaw with his thumb. She drew in a breath, and for a second, he thought she'd ask him to stop. But she didn't. Instead, she leaned her head against his shoulder.

"Thank you for telling me," he said, finally drawing his hand away.

"I'm glad I did. It's nice to not have to keep that to myself any longer. Do you . . . Do you think I should put the rest of the money in the bank? Or should we use it to build the house?"

Matthew closed his eyes at the offer. It was so thoughtful—so unexpected—for her to offer that, especially considering the hastiness of their marriage. But it didn't feel right for him to accept it.

"I think you should put it into the bank. Keep it safe in case it's needed someday," he said.

"All right. I left some of those investments—the ones I couldn't sell quickly enough. If Mr. Durham hasn't somehow convinced the companies that those belong to him, there will be more money to come as soon as I write and request the sale. But I'm not sure if that's a wise decision."

Matthew thought for a moment. It was a careful balance—if she left them for too long, this Durham had more time to weasel his way into the companies' good graces. But if she had them sold and the proceeds sent here . . . What was keeping Durham from discovering their location?

"I'm not certain either," he confessed. "Let's think about it a little more. Maybe there's another way."

"Perhaps the banker, Mr. . . ."

"Gardiner," he supplied.

"Yes, Mr. Gardiner. Perhaps he might have an idea."

It was a good suggestion. "Let's speak with him tomorrow."

They whiled away the last of the afternoon by the creek. Sophia told him about her parents and home in Kansas City, and it was easy to draw parallels between their families. No wonder she seemed to fit in so perfectly with his own family.

The shadows had begun growing longer when they finally headed back up to the hotel for dinner. Sophia wondered aloud at the options that might be on the night's menu, and Matthew laughed out loud as her suggestions grew wilder.

"Pickled eggs with chopped herring and lemon-marinated cheese," she said as they strode down the long hallway that led from the hotel's back door toward the lobby.

"If that actually appears on the menu, I fully expect you to order it." He tried to keep a straight face.

She laid a hand over her heart. "I'd do no such—"

"Pardon me, sir."

Matthew turned to see one of the desk clerks hurrying after him as they approached the door to the dining room.

"This came for you." The man held out what Matthew recognized as a folded telegram message. "The boy tried to deliver it to your home but was informed you were staying here for the night."

"Thank you." Matthew took the telegram, his curiosity piqued. He didn't often receive telegrams. In fact, he could count on one hand the number of times he'd had one delivered, and that was generally in the event of death or urgent land office matters.

"Who is it from?" Sophia asked as they stepped to the side of the doors to allow other diners to enter.

"I'm not certain." He unfolded it, his eyes going immediately to the name at the bottom—and his heart dropped.

Miss D. Timperman.

Chapter Seventeen

AS LOVELY AS THE ROOM at the hotel was, Sophia could not fall asleep.

Matthew, ever the gentleman, had taken up sleeping on the floor to allow her the bed, which had stirred up emotions Sophia hadn't known existed. And that was ridiculous, because *she* was the one who had heartily agreed to the arrangement when he'd proposed marriage. This was what she wanted . . . wasn't it?

When she wasn't thinking about that, the words from Miss Timperman's telegram floated through her mind.

Delayed. Arrival by train in September. Explanation forthcoming.

Yours, D. Timperman

Matthew said he would send her a return telegram tomorrow. If she'd just sent the message, she couldn't have left yet. Yet something about the message set Sophia on edge. Why was Miss Timperman coming now, after so much time? Did she know that Sophia had pretended to be her? Why hadn't she sent Matthew a letter to explain her delay?

Sophia laid in the comfortable bed and stared at the ceiling while the sounds of Matthew breathing quietly rose from the floor beside her. She smiled in the darkness at the sound. Slowly, her eyes began to close, and before she knew it, she was lost in a pleasant dream about a home near a stand of pines, overlooking a wide expanse of the valley.

IT DIDN'T TAKE LONG for Sophia to ease into life at the Canton home. Matthew's parents were welcoming and generous, but to Sophia's great relief, they were never overbearing. Mrs. Canton gratefully accepted Sophia's help in preparing meals, and Sophia soon discovered that dinner guests were more frequent than not. She especially delighted in having the kitchen and ingredients needed to bake again—and the people to enjoy her cakes and cookies and pies.

"I fear my husband will be gravely disappointed once you and Matthew have your own home," Mrs. Canton said one morning when Sophia put the finishing touches on an apple pie.

"Well, then we'll have to make a point of coming to visit often." Sophia put the pie into the oven.

Mrs. Canton wiped down the small countertop. "I don't suppose you enjoy sewing as much as baking?"

Sophia made a face. "Let's just say I can accomplish what needs doing."

"I feel the same way," Mrs. Canton said with a laugh as she draped the cloth to dry. "But it is much more enjoyable when done with friends. Trudie Gardiner is hosting a sewing circle this afternoon. Would you like to come with me?"

Sophia readily agreed. The banker's wife had been present when she and Matthew had gone to deposit the remainder of her money into the bank, her little one in her arms. After Mr.

Gardiner had reassured her of her deposit's safety there and had offered to discreetly contact the companies in Kansas City on her behalf to ensure the investments remained in her name only, Trudie had insisted she come over for tea. Sophia had taken to her immediately. She was a woman without pretense—quick to make a joke and full of wild tales about her time in Chicago, most of which she'd spent as a lady pickpocket.

It was then Sophia realized that Crest Stone was made up of all sorts. If a former pickpocket could become a banker's wife, what else was possible? Suddenly, her own tale seemed to fit right in, and she was eager to get to know all of the ladies. So far, she'd discovered that Caroline Drexel, who ran the mercantile with her husband, had also been running from a terrible man who'd wanted to marry her when she came to Crest Stone, and Edie Wright, the sheriff's wife, had grown up in a family of outlaws.

After the noon meal, Sophia changed quickly into the beautiful yellow dress that the dressmaker had finished for her, wondering what other fascinating stories she might hear today. Then she gathered up some mending and the sewing supplies she'd recently purchased and together, she and Mrs. Canton walked the short distance to the edge of town, where Trudie Gardiner's large home sat almost directly across from the boarding house.

A maid—quite possibly the only one in Crest Stone aside from the ones who worked at the hotel—ushered them into the parlor where several of the ladies from town already sat. Sophia was grateful to see that a few of them had also brought mending. She'd feared she'd be the only one not doing needlepoint or sewing some useful clothing.

Trudie beckoned her to the settee where she already sat while Mrs. Canton took an empty chair next to an older woman with graying brown hair.

"Florence!" Mrs. Canton exclaimed as she took her seat. "What a wonderful surprise to see you here."

"It happened to be my afternoon off work. The hotel dining room will simply have to do without me today," the other woman said with a smile, and Sophia had the impression that afternoons off for Florence weren't very common.

Mrs. Canton launched into questions about the hotel which Florence answered. Sophia's eyes wandered to the other ladies. There were several she'd met already, and a few new faces. She grinned when she saw one of the girls she knew from her time at the boarding house. Deirdre Hannan immediately left her seat and came to sit in the one next to the settee.

"How is life as Mrs. Canton?" Deirdre Hannan asked. She'd lived at the boarding house for several months upon her arrival in town with her brother the summer before. They now lived in a house in town, but Deirdre returned to the Darbys' boarding house for frequent visits with the friends she'd made there.

Sophia couldn't help but smile in response to Deirdre's question. Getting to know Matthew better was something she looked forward to each day. "It's wonderful," she said.

A wistful look crossed Deirdre's face. "I wish I could find someone I loved as much as you love Mr. Canton."

"You will," Sophia said, her face warming a bit at the word *love*. She didn't know if it was quite that—at least not yet—but she certainly enjoyed Matthew's company. And it appeared he felt the same. "I just know you will."

It was hard to figure out why Deirdre hadn't already married. The men in town greatly outnumbered the ladies, hence the mail-order bride business one of the ladies in Crest Stone started with a friend who lived in a nearby town.

"If you reexamine your expectations, that is, Deirdre," Trudie added as she stabbed a needle into a particularly thick looking piece of fabric. "Deirdre is far too choosy. Every man she's met, she's found wanting."

Deirdre shrugged. "I have no wish to be attached to someone I don't find interesting."

"And I can't believe there's not a single man in town that *doesn't* pique your interest," Trudie replied.

At that, Deirdre ducked her head, and Sophia thought for certain she was hiding a smile as she pretended to examine her needlework. But she kept that observation to herself. Trudie seemed the sort to never leave a body alone if she thought she knew something.

A few more ladies arrived, filling in the circle of seating Trudie had set up in her parlor, and the conversation was animated. Sophia found herself laughing on more than one occasion, and the thoughts of Daisy Timperman faded even farther into the distance.

In fact, each day that had passed gave her reassurance that Miss Timperman had received Matthew's telegram. She was likely searching for a new husband by now, and that thought buoyed Sophia's mood. Without worries of Miss Timperman arriving or Mr. Durham finding out where she was and stealing the remainder of her investments, she could put her mind to happier things—like enjoying this sewing circle, talking with

Matthew, and planning for their eventual move to the house he hoped to begin building by the end of summer.

"—alone at the bank."

Sophia's attention turned to Trudie, who was shaking her head as she finished speaking.

"And it's too bad," she continued. "Because I was truly enjoying spending a part of the morning there."

"But why not? I don't see anything disreputable about a woman working alone at a business, at least not out here," Clara Carlisle, the livery owner's wife, said. "I've been at the livery alone more times than I can count when Roman and the others were off delivering carriages and horses."

"It isn't that." Trudie sighed and rested her hands on top of her sewing. "It's this man who came in the day before yesterday. Thankfully, the baby was sleeping in Weston's office. This fellow stormed in and insisted upon talking to my husband—who wasn't there, clearly—and when I told him that, he grew irate and threatened to come around behind the counter and find the information he needed himself."

Sophia's eyes grew round at Trudie's story. It reminded her far too much of her experiences with the bandits who had taken her from the wagon train, but at least they had others with them who stopped anything from getting out of hand. But that man had no one to stop him, except Trudie herself.

"What did you do?" Deirdre practically breathed out the words.

"Well, I told him I'd shoot him if he attempted to step one foot around the counter."

Clara bit her lip to hide a grin, and Sophia guessed this sort of reaction wasn't at all out of character for Trudie.

"You didn't need to . . . did you?" Sophia asked. She couldn't imagine raising a weapon at someone, much less using it. But she supposed that if she'd had a pistol when she'd been with those outlaws, she just might have anyway.

"No, thankfully. Although I showed him I meant what I said." Trudie picked up her sewing and frowned at it. "He was very lucky that another customer arrived when he did. He left, grudgingly."

Deirdre had a hand pressed to her heart. "You don't suppose he's still in town?"

Trudie shrugged. "It's possible. Although I doubt he'd dare return to the bank. Weston won't help him. He'd sooner toss him into the street than allow him to open an account."

"What did he look like?" Clara asked. "I'd hate to have him visit the livery and be unprepared."

"Well, he certainly wasn't handsome," Trudie replied. "He was tall, but when he took off his hat, he was missing the hair on the top of his head. What little he had was light shade of brown. And he was a portly fellow, of the sort who indulges in far too many sweets. His eyes sat oddly, too, as if they were too close together." She shuddered, as if the image repulsed her.

Sophia's heart lurched into her chest.

The man Trudie described sounded exactly like Francis Durham.

Chapter Eighteen

"DID HE GIVE HIS NAME?" Matthew asked as he and Sophia made their way to the mercantile.

"No, he left before she could ask." Sophia looked up at Mathew. "You don't think it could be him?"

Matthew pushed his lips together, thinking. *Could be*, of course. But likely? "I doubt it is. Even if Mrs. Gardiner's description matches, she could be describing any number of men. And don't you think he would have come around asking for you by now?"

The worry still sat in Sophia's eyes, though.

"How about if I speak to the marshal, just in case," he suggested.

That seemed to ease Sophia's mind. She nodded. "At least this is a small town. If he's here, he can't hide for long."

Matthew laughed. "That's true. I still suspect that man was merely a troublemaker, passing through. I imagine he's already headed out of town, on his way to try to rob a bank somewhere else."

"Do you suppose that was what he was trying to do?" Sophia's eyes were as round as the full moon.

"It seems the most likely." He gripped her elbow as they stepped over the railroad tracks, just as the train's whistle sounded from a distance. "Look." He pointed down the tracks toward the north.

Sophia lifted a hand to shade her eyes. "I really ought to have spent the money to come by train."

"But then you never would have met me." Matthew gave her a smile as they finished crossing the road and stepped up onto the board sidewalk.

"Oh, that is true." She studied his face a moment. "Hmm . . . travel with the comfort of a seat and make the journey in a fraction of the time, or take a dusty wagon to be kidnapped by outlaws and rescued by a handsome man . . ." She put a finger to her lips as if she were considering the options.

"That's the second time you've told me I'm handsome." He grinned at her.

"Well . . ." Her face went pink.

"I don't see a contest there at all. I believe I win, solely on my good looks." He bit the inside of his cheek as he began walking toward the mercantile, her arm safely ensconced around his.

"Why, Matthew Canton, I never pegged you as a pompous sort of man." Her voice was light and teasing, and he thought he'd do anything to keep her from thinking of Mr. Durham ever again.

"Then I suppose you still have a lot to learn." He adjusted a nonexistent monocle and puffed out his chest as if he thought himself the king of Crest Stone, Colorado.

Her laugh rang like bells, and Matthew couldn't keep the smile from his face.

Just as they approached the mercantile, a pile of packages blocked the sidewalk. "Pardon me," the woman standing next to them said. "My husband's gone for the wagon."

"It's quite all right," Matthew replied. He led Sophia off the sidewalk, onto the stretch of empty land that ran between the mercantile and the building they'd just passed. The ground was rougher than he'd expected, with the dips and rises hidden by long grasses.

"Careful," he said—just as Sophia let out a little squeak.

Her toe caught against a low spot in the dirt as she tipped forward. In a split second, Matthew stepped in front of her as he gripped her arm tighter. His other hand caught her around the waist and instead of falling face first onto the ground, she fell straight against his chest.

"Are you all right?" he asked.

It took a second, but Sophia nodded. "I think so." She looked up at him, her soft brown eyes framed with long, dark lashes. Freckles from the long days spent on the wagon train dotted her cheeks, and Matthew was seized with the desire to trace the distance between them with his finger. But that was impossible because . . . well, because he was essentially holding her to him.

He ought to set her upright. They were just off the public street, after all. Anyone who strode by on the sidewalk would be able to see them. If that lady waiting for her husband turned around—

"Thank you." The breath from her sweet words caressed his face, and Matthew no longer cared who was standing on the sidewalk or what anyone from town might think. All he could think about was Sophia—Sophia's lovely face, her breath coming quickly against his cheek, the feel of her against him, her pink lips.

He leaned his face just ever so slightly closer to hers. She didn't pull away. Instead, her breath seemed to catch in her throat, and her eyes fluttered closed. Did she want him to kiss her? His heart beat wildly and his thoughts spun. Oh, how he *wanted* to kiss her.

He moved even closer, until he was but a fraction of an inch away. This was different from their wedding. That chaste little kiss had been wonderful, but awkward. He'd held back every thought or feeling he had then. But now . . .

He couldn't have held them back if he wanted to.

He tightened his grip around her, and she sighed. His eyes closed, and the sounds of the town disappeared as he began to close the short distance between them.

She sighed again—a breath gracing his mouth—and just as he pressed against her, a raindrop splattered on his nose.

"Oh!" Sophia's eyes flew open the same time as Matthew's did. More raindrops fell, fat drops of water that splashed on their faces and against their clothing.

She lifted a hand to her hat, as if that would protect it from the rain, and Matthew looked up to the sky. There, one single dark cloud marred the blue expanse. He couldn't help but laugh.

"What's so funny?" Sophia said as he helped her back onto the sidewalk.

He grinned at her as they darted into the mercantile. "I think God was trying to protect both our reputations."

She smiled back at him. "In that case, I'm a little upset with God." Then she turned to Caroline Drexel who was nearby arranging a shelf of merchandise, leaving Matthew to laugh again.

And he couldn't wait for a more private opportunity to try that kiss again.

Chapter Nineteen

MONDAYS WERE ALWAYS something of a disappointment.

But perhaps that was because Sundays were so enjoyable. The land office was closed, and Sophia so loved Sunday dinner at the Canton home. There were never fewer then four or five guests, with plenty of food and good company. And although she didn't go looking for compliments on her baking, everyone seemed to praise her dessert creations. Afterward, there was plenty of time for her and Matthew to take a walk around town or drive out to his land or visit Silver Creek.

Sophia had hoped he might try to kiss her again yesterday, but it had seemed half the town had the same idea for a stroll along the creek. And he always stayed up later than she did, presumably to allow her to fall asleep without interruption—although lately she'd wondered if there might be other reasons.

Color rose to her cheeks just thinking about that, and she busied herself with a hearty sweeping of the kitchen. Mrs. Canton had gone to the new butcher shop that had recently opened, and the reverend was visiting a family on a farm outside of town. The house felt strangely empty with no one around, and the silence drove a restless energy inside her.

Just as she was about to give up on the sweeping and find a reason to go to the mercantile or the boarding house, a knock came at the door. Someone must have read her mind, she thought as she leaned the broom against the wall and walked to the door.

Outside the Cantons' home stood a tall, willowy woman about Sophia's own age. Her pale hair was drawn back tightly in a style that made Sophia's own head ache to contemplate. Her blue eyes flicked from Sophia to the interior of the house behind her.

"Good afternoon," Sophia said pleasantly. "The reverend is out at the moment, but if you'd like, you can wait for him in the parlor. I expect he'll return in an hour or so. If you're hungry, we have tea and cookies." She bit her lip before she could say more. She'd probably scared this poor girl away with her eagerness for company. She opened the door wider in invitation.

The woman stepped inside with a nervous smile. She brought with her a battered carpetbag that Sophia hadn't noticed before.

"Oh, have you just arrived in town?" Sophia held out her hand for the woman's bag and traveling cloak.

"I have," she said, in a thin, uncertain voice. "Thank you." She handed her things to Sophia, who hung the cloak on the coatrack and set the bag on the floor beneath it.

"Well, then, you must be exhausted. Come sit down, and I'll bring you some refreshments." Sophia gestured to the parlor.

The woman entered, her gaze wandering about the room before she turned back to Sophia. "I'm sorry. I should have asked your name. Are you the Cantons' maid?"

Sophia choked back a giggle. "No, although I can see how you could come to that conclusion. I'm Sophia Canton." She didn't think she'd ever get used to the little bolt of excitement that shot through her at the use of her new last name. She couldn't help but smile every time she used it. "May I ask yours?"

"I'm Daisy Timperman. I was supposed to be here some time ago, but . . . well . . . Are you all right, Miss Canton?"

Sophia's fingers dug into the doorframe as she pasted a smile onto her face. "Mrs. Canton," she said out of a lack of anything else to say. "Why don't I fetch us those refreshments?"

Before Miss Timperman could respond, Sophia was gone, throwing herself into the kitchen where she grabbed hold of the back of the nearest chair and tried to catch her breath.

Daisy Timperman was here. She was *here*.

And she was expecting to marry Matthew.

Chapter Twenty

SOPHIA MET MATTHEW at the door with wide eyes and a pale face.

He stopped still, just outside the door. Perhaps it was a good thing he'd come home early. "What is it?"

She glanced behind her, and then whispered, "She's here."

He knew immediately who she meant—but he couldn't believe it. "She? You can't mean . . ."

"Miss Timperman."

He closed his eyes briefly. "How long has she been here?"

"Less than an hour. I . . . I couldn't tell her. I'm sorry. She looks as if she'll break in two at bad news." Sophia twisted her hands together.

He nodded. It was his responsibility anyway.

"Your mother just returned home too. She's with Miss Timperman now, but I doubt she's said anything since I've been gone."

He placed a hand on each of Sophia's arms. "Why don't you take a rest? Or go for a visit? I'll talk to her."

"I could do with a walk," she said.

He leaned forward and kissed her forehead. She rewarded him with a momentary smile. "Go. When you return, she'll be gone."

Sophia darted out the door as if she couldn't get away fast enough. Matthew pushed his shoulders back and entered. The moment he appeared in the doorway to the parlor, his mother stood.

"There he is. Matthew, Miss Timperman has arrived." She gave him a look that could have melted butter in January. "I'll leave you two to talk."

As she passed, Matthew leaned over and whispered into her ear. "I'll explain later."

"I'll expect it. Poor Sophia was awfully brave," she said under her breath.

When Mama had retreated to the kitchen, Matthew entered the room. "Good afternoon," he said stiffly. What was the protocol for this odd situation? He didn't know whether to sit or stand, much less what to do with his hands.

She gave him a smile that was more timid than warm. "Good afternoon, Mr. Canton. Please sit. I'm so happy to finally meet you."

"I . . ." He sat, and then stood immediately again. He was far too nervous to remain in one place. "I didn't know you were coming," he said lamely as he crossed to the hearth, cold now in the heat of summer.

"I sent a telegram."

When he turned around, her brow was furrowed, and his heart hurt at what would surely be her disappointment. "I received it, and I sent one in return."

"I must have missed it. I left rather quickly after I sent mine." She stood then, pressing her hands into the sides of her well-worn dress. "I owe you apologies. I . . . Well, to be honest, I let my fears overcome me. And then I was too embarrassed to admit that to you, and so I didn't write—and I didn't come with the wagon train."

Matthew held up a hand. "There's no need to explain. I must—"

"No, please!" She took a step forward, desperation crossing her face so quickly that Matthew swallowed his words and lowered his hand. "Let me explain myself. I was wrong, and I realized that I really did wish to marry you even if leaving home scared me. So I summoned my courage and sent that telegram after I'd sold some of my things to raise enough money to supplement what my parents gave me to buy a train ticket. And . . ." She lifted her arms. "Here I am."

Here she was. And now Matthew had to tell her that he couldn't marry her.

"Miss Timperman—"

"Daisy, please. If we are to be married, you must call me Daisy." She gave him a shy smile that made him feel like the worst man on earth.

"Miss Timperman," he said firmly. Clasping his hands behind his back, he pulled the words he needed to say from where they'd seemed stuck in his mind. "I cannot marry you. I'm sorry you came all this way, but that was what I'd relayed in my telegram."

Her mouth opened slightly, and she began to shake her head as if she could erase the words he'd just said.

He swallowed hard and forced himself to keep going. "I am truly sorry you went to the effort and expense to come here. And I'm even more sorry if I'm causing you any distress, but the fact remains that we can't be married."

Her jaw worked, and for a moment, he feared she might cry. Her eyes went watery, and she looked down at the floor. "Is there something about me that— that you don't like?"

"No!" he said quickly, not wishing to hurt her even further. Not a woman in the world could match Sophia's grace and wit and the way she looked at him with those beautiful eyes. Miss Timperman was not Sophia, but she certainly wasn't an ogre. "No, of course not." He had to tell her. There would be no way around it. "You see, I'm already married."

Her head jerked up, eyes wide. "To whom?"

"The lady you met earlier."

"Mrs. Canton." She looked away, shaking her head. When she turned her attention back to him, her features had narrowed slightly. Gone was the sadness, and in its place . . . Was that resignation? An attempt to salvage dignity? Anger? Matthew couldn't tell for certain.

"I should have known," she said in a sharper voice. "You never wrote." When he looked at her in confusion, she added, "When I didn't arrive. You never wrote to find out why or to ask if all was well."

He simply stared at her.

"I suppose it didn't matter to you since you'd already found someone to replace me." Her voice was cold, and Matthew reminded himself it was because she was hurt.

He opted to ignore her barbs and instead gestured toward the door. "Why don't I escort you to the boarding house? It's a nice place to stay. If you wish—"

"And now you're trying to get me out of your house?" She shook her head. "This is unbelievable. I can see myself out, thank you." She brushed past him into the hallway.

Matthew pressed his fingers to the bridge of his nose, trying to ward off an oncoming headache, before turning around. Miss Timperman was gathering her cloak and bag.

"Do you need money for the boarding house? Or for the train home?" Such an expense would set back his plans to begin building by the end of summer, but it was the gentlemanly thing to do. He could hardly leave the woman stranded here if she wished to return to Missouri.

But she looked aghast at his suggestion. "I don't need your *money*!"

And with that, she swept out the door. She paused a moment, lifted her chin, and added, "I wish you and Mrs. Canton a good life." Then she was gone.

Matthew closed his eyes, half in relief and half in utter exhaustion.

"Are you all right?" Mama's voice sounded from the hallway behind him.

He opened his eyes and turned around. "As well as I can be. Thank you for entertaining her."

Mama nodded and peered around him. "I hope that poor girl knows where the boarding house is." She drew her gaze back to him. "Why don't you sit down in the kitchen? Have some tea and a slice of Sophia's bread."

He couldn't face the questions he knew Mama would have waiting for him. Perhaps it was better if he just went back to work. "I need to get back to the office." He paused. "When Sophia returns, please tell her I'll be home at my usual time."

Mama nodded, and Matthew exited the house. Far down the road, he caught a glimpse of Miss Timperman, heading in the opposite direction from the boarding house. Well, at least

Crest Stone was small enough that once she reached that edge of town, she wouldn't have far to walk to get to the other end, where the boarding house sat.

He pulled his hat on and started across the street to ensure he didn't run into her on his way to the land office. A hundred different emotions swirled through him. He hadn't done wrong—that much he knew. What was he supposed to think when she didn't arrive and sent no explanation? Even Miss Timperman admitted she'd changed her mind. That meant he—and Miss Timperman too—were free of their obligations to one another. And then he'd replied to her telegram as quickly as he could to prevent this exact situation.

He knew it wasn't his fault, and yet he couldn't help feeling as if he'd done something wrong. Perhaps Jake Gilbert would have some advice. Gilbert was more of a friend than a boss, and he'd been the one to refer Matthew to his wife's mail-order bride advertising business when Matthew first mentioned his wish to marry.

But when Matthew pressed open the door to the land office, Jake spoke up first.

"Oh, good, you're back." He came around from behind the big table in the middle of the room. "There was a man in here just a while ago asking after you."

Matthew raised his eyebrows. He hadn't been expecting anyone. "Did he leave a name?"

"He didn't. Seemed aggravated to find you gone though." Gilbert scowled. "Hope he isn't a friend of yours. If he'd stayed a second longer, he would've found himself pushed out that door—if I was feeling kind, anyway."

Matthew couldn't think of a friend who'd be so belligerent as to rattle Jake Gilbert, who was a normally affable man. "He didn't say what he wanted?"

Jake shook his head. "Only wanted to talk to you. He was a large fellow, tall, round. Oddly set eyes."

Well, that was certainly strange. There was no business at the land office that Gilbert couldn't handle instead of Matthew. And that description fit no one Matthew knew.

"I suppose if it's important, he'll return," Matthew said. He took his hat off and laid it on his desk.

"Let's hope not," Gilbert replied darkly. Then he tilted his head. "Why are you back? I thought you'd left for the day."

Matthew sighed and fell into the chair behind his desk. "Now that's a story."

Gilbert raised his eyebrows. "I'm curious."

And Matthew launched into what he'd found when he had gone home. Telling Jake made it somehow feel less awful. He even offered to ask his wife to befriend Miss Timperman if she was unable to leave town, and perhaps even find her work up at the hotel.

All would be well. But as he returned to his work, Matthew found it wasn't Miss Timperman on his mind, but the angry man who'd come looking for him. Who could he have been?

And what did he want?

Chapter Twenty-one

THE FOLLOWING DAY, Matthew lingered at home before leaving for the land office.

"Perhaps I should take the day off from work," he said, holding Sophia's hand in the hallway near the door.

"There is no need. Miss Timperman is hardly going to come here and yell at me for marrying you," she said with a little smile. Just thinking of the thin blonde woman shrieking at her felt so out of character with the Miss Timperman Sophia had met yesterday that it was hard not to laugh.

"I don't know about that," he replied. "You didn't see how angry she was with me."

"It was merely wounded pride." Sophia squeezed his hand. "She's now had time to think on what's happened, and I imagine she's trying now to secure funds for train fare home. I doubt she ever wants to see you or me again."

After a moment, he nodded. "You're right. I only wish she'd taken me up on my offer to pay the fare for her."

"Then she'd feel as if she owed you." She glanced at the clock in the parlor. "You ought to get to work before Mr. Gilbert starts to worry."

He leaned forward and kissed the top of her head. When he lingered, she thought perhaps now was finally the moment.

Perhaps he'd lift her chin and kiss her in the way she'd been thinking about ever since that moment outside of the mercantile. His eyes searched her face, and just as she thought it might happen, the sound of his mother's humming floated down the hallway from the kitchen.

He chuckled as she sighed, and he brushed the side of her face with his hand instead. "I may ask Jake if he and Mrs. Gilbert would like to join us for dinner."

"That would be wonderful," Sophia said as she pushed away the disappointment. "I'll let your mother know."

The day passed as most others did, and when Sophia left in the afternoon to purchase eggs from a woman in town who kept chickens, she found Miss Timperman watching her from across the road.

No, that was silly. Why would Miss Timperman be *watching* her? Surely it was a coincidence. But after another minute, and several steps later, Sophia glanced across the street again. Sure enough, Miss Timperman was there.

She could either ignore her and pretend it wasn't happening—or she could acknowledge the woman. The latter felt far preferable—and much more likely to put a stop to whatever reason Miss Timperman had for looking at her.

Sophia raised a hand in greeting.

Miss Timperman did not do the same. Instead, she placed her hands on her hips, stared at Sophia for half a moment longer, and then turned and continued on her way.

Sophia pressed her lips together. She'd done nothing at all to Miss Timperman—aside from marrying Matthew. Well, and taking her place on the wagon train, which Miss Timperman likely didn't know about. And if she did, what did it matter?

It wasn't as if those wagons were going to wait weeks for their original guest to change her mind.

No, it had to be jealousy. Pure, simple jealousy. Miss Timperman wished to marry Matthew, and now she couldn't. So she was angry at Matthew and jealous of Sophia.

A tingle of guilt bit at Sophia's heart as she adjusted the basket hanging from her arm. It was her fault Miss Timperman couldn't have the husband she'd intended to have.

But was it, though? Even if Sophia hadn't arrived and met Matthew, he could have gone on to marry any number of women in Miss Timperman's place. Perhaps he would have met someone in Pueblo. Or reconsidered one of the few eligible ladies in Crest Stone.

In her heart, Sophia empathized with Miss Timperman's plight. Here she was, essentially stranded in a strange town, with her prospects entirely changed. Too proud to accept funds to return home. And, apparently, too upset to understand the situation and accept how it had changed.

Miss Timperman weighed heavily on Sophia's heart that evening and into the next day. When she'd told Matthew and his parents about her, Reverend Canton suggested they all pray for her. And Mrs. Canton indicated that Matthew should find a way to make her accept the money for train fare. Sophia thought both ideas were excellent—yet neither seemed to work.

Each time she left the house, she saw Miss Timperman.

Going to the mercantile, visiting with Deirdre, bringing Matthew lunch at his office, even simply taking laundry outside to hang. Her empathy began to fray into irritation.

Hanging the last of the linens, Sophia determined to walk across the road and speak with Miss Timperman. As much as she wanted to demand the woman leave, she thought perhaps another, more gentle approach might get her further. She could offer to introduce her to some of the other ladies in town, ask if she needed help finding work, or invite her to Sunday's church service.

But just as she picked up her laundry basket, Miss Timperman found her instead.

Sophia nearly dropped her basket at the woman's sudden appearance. "Good afternoon." She pushed a smile onto her face, remembering what she'd planned to do.

"It's no such thing." Miss Timperman crossed her arms, and Sophia was reminded of a child who'd grown angry about not getting her own way.

"I'm—I'm sorry." Sophia didn't much know what else to say to that. So she let it go, and summoned up one of her ideas. "I'm glad you're here. I wanted to ask if you'd like to join our sewing circle. It's an informal thing that one of the ladies in town hosts once a week."

Miss Timperman sniffed, her face wrinkled up as if the very idea of spending time sewing with Sophia made her feel ill.

Sophia clenched her jaw. *Try another.* She needed patience—and to remember how Miss Timperman felt. She clutched the edges of the laundry basket and asked, "Have you been able to find work?"

"Why would you care? I'd have thought you'd want me gone from town."

That was something. Not a particularly nice something, but a place from which to start. "No, not at all," Sophia said, the white lie sliding through her lips. "And having been a woman on my own far from home, I understand how much the security of an income can mean. If you haven't found a position, perhaps I could be of assistance."

Miss Timperman's eyebrows slanted down. "I don't want your pity, Mrs. Canton."

Sophia forced a breath in and out. Her patience was fading quickly. "I don't pity you. I've been in a similar—"

"Oh! So you've had your betrothed swept away by another woman, leaving you penniless and alone in a wild, remote town far from home? I'm sorry. I misunderstood!" Miss Timperman's voice took on a sickly, sweet quality that sent every bit of patience Sophia had remaining flying toward the mountains.

She set the basket down. "Now, wait a moment. I was only trying to be friendly and helpful. If you're going to be rude, I'll kindly ask you to leave my home."

"*Your* home?" Miss Timperman's eyebrows disappeared into her hair. "I was under the impression that this belonged to Matthew's parents."

It wasn't lost on Sophia that Miss Timperman had called Matthew by his given name, as if she still held some sort of claim on him. She chose to ignore that. "It does."

"And, tell me, Mrs. Canton, what did the reverend and his wife think when they learned you stole their son's money and pretended to be me?"

So she did know. "They understood my situation," Sophia said calmly. Another thought occurred to her. "How did you find out?"

"Talk around town," Miss Timperman said in a way that made Sophia wonder *who* was talking about her. And whether it was as bad as Miss Timperman made it sound.

No. She was angry, that was all. And she'd use whatever she could to let Sophia know that. Which she'd accomplished, and now, Sophia decided, it was past time for her to leave.

"I'm sorry, I must go in now." Sophia picked up her basket again and stepped to the side to go around the other woman.

But Miss Timperman blocked her path. "Not before you hear what I have to say."

Sophia gritted her teeth. She'd already heard. What else could Miss Timperman possibly have to say?

"Matthew was supposed to be *my* husband, not yours." Miss Timperman pointed a finger at Sophia to emphasize her words. "And I don't give up easily. If I were you, I'd ask him for an annulment today. Then pack your things and leave."

Sophia blinked at her. It was the most preposterous suggestion she'd ever heard. And after she'd tried and tried again to give Miss Timperman the benefit of the doubt. Why, she'd even defended her to Matthew! "No," she said, simply but firmly.

A little smile curled Miss Timperman's lips, but it wasn't friendly at all. In fact, it had an almost cruel slant to it. Chills prickled Sophia's skin, and she gripped the basket even tighter.

"If you don't do as I suggest, you'll be very sorry," Miss Timperman said.

The woman had clearly taken leave of her senses. "What does that mean?"

"It means exactly what I said. You'll wish you *had* annulled this marriage and left town." And with that, Miss Timperman turned on her heel and left.

Sophia stared after her. What had just happened?

Miss Timperman had threatened her. She ought to have laughed it off, but there was something in the woman's voice and the way she looked at Sophia that made the threat seem very, very real.

And very dangerous.

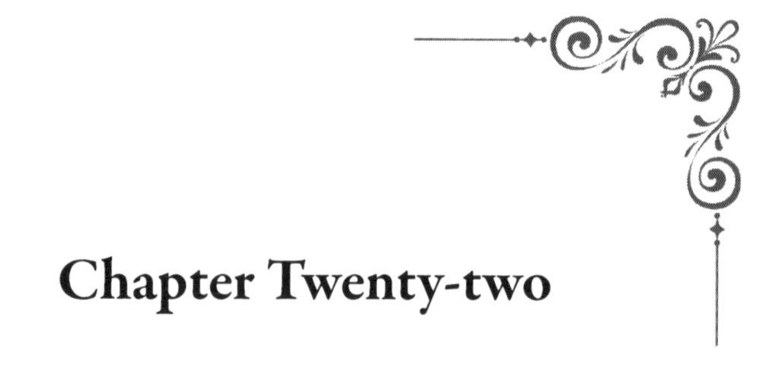

Chapter Twenty-two

SOPHIA'S RECOUNTING of the events that had taken place behind the Cantons' home replayed through Matthew's mind as he made his way to the boarding house that evening. He didn't want to believe it—that Miss Timperman had threatened Sophia—but Sophia was insistent that was exactly what had happened.

Sophia had been so certain just a few days ago that Miss Timperman was simply brokenhearted. But if what the woman had said to her was true, she was more than sad. More than angry even.

And Matthew was determined to put an end to all of it.

He lifted his hand to open the Darbys' boarding house door when a voice called his name. Turning, he found exactly the person for whom he was searching.

"Miss Timperman," he said, his voice kind but businesslike.

"Matthew." She gave him a brilliant smile. "It's so good to see you."

Calling him by his given name aside, her manner was entirely pleasant and polite. He didn't know what he'd expected—a snarling, angry banshee, perhaps—but this certainly wasn't it. He made his way down the boarding house steps and tugged on the brim of his hat in greeting. "Miss Timperman. I trust you're doing well?"

"I am, although much better now that I'm talking with you." Her smile faltered just a little.

He waited a second, bracing for the anger that Sophia said Miss Timperman had unleashed on her. But Miss Timperman's smile reappeared as if she'd threatened exactly no one earlier that day.

"My wife said you paid her a visit this afternoon," he said carefully.

Her smile twitched again, and then fell away. He dug his nails into his palms, waiting.

"I did. I thought . . . well, I suppose I hoped we might become friends." She clasped her hands and looked down. "But I don't believe she wishes to be my friend."

Matthew furrowed his brow. "What do you mean?"

"I'm not a gossip, Matthew. I don't like to tell tales or speak ill of anyone, but this time . . ." She shook her head. "Mrs. Canton was so rude to me that I hardly knew what to say or do. She told me that if I didn't leave town immediately, she'd see to it that I'd regret staying." She looked up at him then, her eyes rimmed in watery tears.

And Matthew didn't know what to think. "That's . . . . Surely you misunderstood. She told me that you said something similar to her."

Miss Timperman pressed a hand to her heart. "If I offended her in any way, I didn't mean to. I don't know how I would have, though. I didn't mean to cause her any distress."

"I . . . I'll tell her." Matthew stood awkwardly, shoving his hands into his trousers pockets.

"Well, good night, then." She gave him another bright smile before climbing the steps and going into the boarding house.

Matthew stared at the closed door. He didn't know what had happened now. He believed Sophia, but perhaps she had misinterpreted Miss Timperman's words. And as irritated as he'd been with Miss Timperman's reaction upon learning he'd married Sophia, it was difficult to imagine her threatening Sophia—just as it was impossible to imagine Sophia doing the same to Miss Timperman.

They must have misunderstood one another.

Feeling more certain in his assessment, Matthew left the boarding house.

When he reached home, he found Sophia outside, sitting in a rocking chair on the back porch and reading a newspaper. He smiled at the image before him. It seemed each day Sophia surprised him with some new, fascinating aspect of her personality. "I didn't know you took an interest in the newspapers."

She looked up, her smile as lovely as ever. Unlike Miss Timperman's grin, Sophia's felt like home. The moment he saw it, Matthew felt at ease, as if he could finally shed the cares of the day and rest his feet.

"I like to know what's happening in the world," she said, setting the paper on the little wooden table next to the rocker. She stood and met him at the porch steps. "How did you find Miss Timperman? Was she remorseful or angry?"

Matthew leaned against the nearby column. "I believe this was all a misunderstanding between the two of you."

Sophia lifted her eyebrows. "I most certainly didn't *misunderstand* that she said I'd regret it mightily if I didn't seek to annul our marriage."

Matthew drew in a breath. He didn't want to anger her. Both women seemed set on what they thought they'd heard. He only wanted peace between them, especially considering it seemed Miss Timperman wasn't leaving anytime soon.

"She misheard what you said, too. She thought you threatened her if she didn't leave town." He spoke carefully, hoping Sophia would see what had most likely happened.

But instead, her eyes narrowed and she straightened. "Do you believe her words over mine?"

"No, I don't," he said honestly. "But I don't think she meant you any harm. Just as I know you didn't mean her harm."

Sophia shook her head slowly, as if she couldn't believe what he was saying. "No, what I said was true. You weren't here. The way she said it . . . it wasn't just the words she spoke. I had goosepimples from the way she looked at me, Matthew. Did you convince her to leave?"

He paused before he spoke. "I didn't ask her to. After she told me what she thought had happened, I saw the misunderstanding—"

"It *wasn't* a misunderstanding." Sophia clenched her hands at her sides. "Don't you remember how angry she was when she found out we were married?"

"Yes, and you convinced me to give her the benefit of the doubt. Sophia . . . I believe you may have to ask that of yourself now." He reached out for her hand, but she stepped away.

"No. I won't do that. Not after she came here and—and—" She let out a breath of frustration. "I can't believe you wouldn't insist she leave after what she said."

He sighed. This was not going the way he'd hoped, not at all. "Perhaps it might be best if the two of you simply avoid one another."

Sophia threw up her hands. "How am I supposed to do that if she shows up unannounced and follows me and *threatens* me?"

"She didn't mean to, and I honestly wonder if she just happened to be in the same places you were around town."

"I did *not* imagine it." She stared at him a moment, her expression changing almost instantly from annoyance to disbelief. She wrapped her arms around herself. "You didn't ask her to leave town?"

"No. I thought . . ." What *did* he think? That it was rude to force her to go, to insist she humble herself and take his money? It seemed so wrong after her disappointment in arriving here to find him married. But her ongoing presence clearly bothered Sophia, even if she had been nothing but kind and welcoming and understanding at first. And could he blame her? He began to second guess his decision not to insist to Miss Timperman that she return home.

"You thought that you wished you'd married her as you'd intended." Sophia finished his sentence for him, her words so quiet that Matthew almost thought he'd imagined them.

But that accusing look in her eyes said otherwise.

"No," he said, taking a step toward her. "Of course not. Why would you think that?"

"It makes perfect sense. Why you've defended her. Why you don't believe me. Why would you? After all, I was deceiving you when you first met me. At least Miss Timperman was honest, even if she did change her mind—twice."

"Sophia." He reached for her arm, but she shook it away, stepping out of his grasp toward the door.

"Please don't touch me." She gulped, half hiccup and half sob. "This was too good to be true. I should have known it."

"It isn't. I don't want Miss Timperman. I want *you*." His voice strained on the last word, desperate to let her know how he felt.

But she shook her head. "That's why you haven't tried to kiss me again. That's why you won't make her leave."

"That's why I . . ." He ran a hand over his face, trying to make sense of her words. "I was trying to respect the agreement we'd made when we married. To give you time. And we have no privacy here. And— Sophia!"

But she'd gone inside.

He pulled the door open just in time to see the door to their bedroom shut. He paused outside it, trying the door only to find it locked. "Sophia!"

"Leave me be. *Please*, Matthew."

"I'd rather talk to you," he said through the closed door, bracing a hand against it.

But she didn't answer. He called her name again, but only silence ensued.

"Matthew." Mama stood in the doorway to the kitchen. "Give her time. Talk to her once she's had a good cry."

"I don't . . . I was trying to do the right thing. But it was wrong." *It was all wrong.*

Mama nodded. "Marriage is hard. Leave her be for a while, and then together you'll figure it out. I promise." She slipped back into the kitchen.

Matthew stared at the closed bedroom door. *Give her time.* It was sound advice.

But something inside told him time was the one thing he didn't have.

He shook away that thought. He'd go for a walk. And then he'd come back and maybe then she'd speak with him, and he'd convince her that she was the only one he wanted. It would work.

It *had* to work. Because if she gave up on him, he wasn't certain he'd ever be all right again.

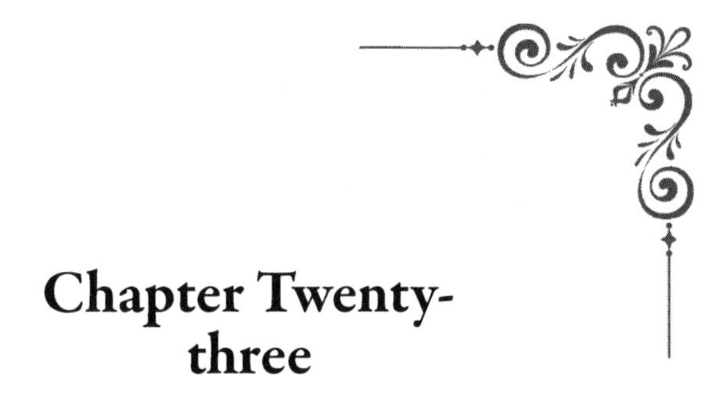

Chapter Twenty-three

MIDMORNING THE NEXT day, Sophia finally emerged from the bedroom to a silent, empty house. She was grateful for that, at least. Her single bag was packed, and it was easier to leave without having to face Reverend and Mrs. Canton. Saying goodbye to them might break her resolve entirely.

Part of her wished to run back into the room and wait for Matthew to return. To beg him to love her and to send Miss Timperman away.

She squared her shoulders and shut the door behind her. She'd already asked him to convince Miss Timperman to go, and he had chosen not to. Not only that, he didn't believe her when she said the woman had threatened her.

Well, Miss Timperman had won. Sophia would leave, and once she arrived to wherever she might end up, she'd find an attorney to annul her marriage. Matthew would be free to marry the woman he wanted to marry all along.

And Sophia would be alone again.

She crept through the quiet house, trying not to think again about his betrayal. That had hurt most of all. She thought he'd understood that she was sorry to have deceived him when they'd first met, but it seemed he had never truly forgiven her. And she had only herself to blame for that.

Stepping outside, Sophia closed the door and began to make her way to the bank. She would withdraw her money and then leave on the noon train. It headed south, she thought, toward Santa Fe. New Mexico Territory sounded as good a place as any. Or perhaps she'd continue on to California.

Wherever she went, it wouldn't be the same. But it would be hers, and that would have to be good enough.

She was all the way to the boarding house before she realized she'd not only passed the bank, but was on the wrong side of the road. She turned to make her way back—and ran right into someone.

Not just *someone*.

Mr. Durham.

Sophia gasped as his hand shot out to grab hold of her arm. "Let go—"

"There's no need for hysterics, Miss Zane. Or wait, it's Mrs. Canton now, isn't it? Didn't want to marry me, but you'll throw yourself at the first man who comes your way out here."

All the distaste Sophia had felt for him back in Kansas City resurfaced, rising from deep inside and finding its way out through words. "How dare you. Take your hand off me, Mr. Durham, or I'll be forced to make a scene out here on the street."

"There's no need for that, Mrs. Canton." He dropped his eyes to the bag at her side. "Are you leaving? How convenient."

She didn't answer. He was almost certainly the man Trudie had described causing trouble in the bank. And if he knew she was here and he had been in the bank, that meant he wanted one thing.

Her money.

She had to talk to him. To keep him distracted long enough for someone to see them and take note of her distress. "How did you find me?"

An ugly grin overtook his face. "It took some effort, but I'm persistent. Once I determined you were no longer in the city and no one at the depot had seen you, all I could figure was that you'd gone out with a wagon train. And sure enough, a man who'd grown ill and had to remain behind told me all about the lady on her own who'd arrived just before the wagons left. She had a different name, but she fit your description." His fingers dug into her arm. "I must hand it to you. I never figured you as one to endure a journey by covered wagon."

Sophia lifted her chin. "There is a lot about me you don't know, Mr. Durham."

He made a sound in his throat, as if he was strangling a laugh. "I'm only here to claim what is rightfully mine. What you stole from me. I want the money, Mrs. Canton."

"You're too late," she said. "It's gone." Her heart thumped harder. It was partially true. *Some* of the money was gone, paid to outlaws and spent on train fare and lodging and two new dresses.

His grip loosened just a little as he regarded her. "You're lying." He shook his head. "It makes me awfully glad I didn't marry you." He said this as if he'd been the one to make that decision.

I am not a liar. Sophia repeated the words to herself, even though she knew deep in her heart that was why Matthew had chosen Miss Timperman over herself. It didn't matter how much she had apologized for pretending to be Miss Timperman—it hadn't been enough.

And so she didn't square her shoulders and insist she was telling the truth. It wouldn't have mattered anyway. Mr. Durham was going on about meeting someone in the saloon who'd told him that he'd seen Sophia and Matthew at the bank making a large deposit.

"I believe it's time you accompany *me* to the bank," Mr. Durham said, leaning closer to her.

No one was nearby to help her. Before she could respond, he'd begun walking across the road, forcing her to come with him.

"You might be able to make me come with you, but I won't speak. And no one at the bank will withdraw those funds without my consent," she said as she tried to keep up with him. "And I'll scream if you drag me any farther."

He stopped—right there in the middle of the road, just past the railroad tracks—and turned. He yanked her closer, withdrawing a small pistol from his pocket. She gasped as he pressed it to her stomach. "You will come with me and say exactly what I tell you to or you'll lose your husband to my partner. And your life too, so suppose that won't really matter, will it?"

Sophia blinked at him, trying to make sense of his words while trying to ignore the feel of that small revolver against her dress. He had a partner . . . Someone else who was working with him. Who was helping him. And she would lose her husband to . . . Her eyes widened as the answer came to her. It was impossible, and yet it was the only thing that made sense.

He laughed as he watched her face. "Yes, poor sad Miss Timperman. It was fairly easy to convince her to help me if she got the only thing she wanted in return."

Sophia said nothing. He didn't know that she'd already lost Matthew to Miss Timperman. He didn't know she had nothing at all left to lose, save the money in the bank.

He pulled her across the remainder of the street. Sophia didn't fight him.

She had nothing left to fight for.

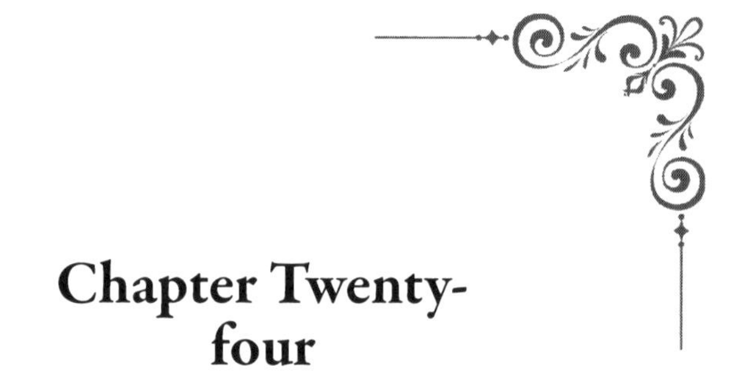

Chapter Twenty-four

MISS TIMPERMAN APPEARED like a ghost in the doorway of the land office.

Matthew groaned inwardly when he saw her. When would the woman realize he was no longer an option for her?

"Miss Timperman." He stood and strode across the room as Jake Gilbert watched him curiously from the table where he was discussing a potential sale of property with a customer.

"Good morning, Matthew." That beaming smile was back.

He closed the space between them and gestured at the door. She took his hint and stepped outside. Matthew shut the door behind them, leaving Gilbert to conduct his business in peace.

"Do you need something?" It was best, he decided, to get to the point with her. A part of him hoped she'd changed her mind about accepting his help to return home.

"Oh, not a thing! Although I am sorry about Mrs. Canton."

Matthew paused. "What do you mean?"

"Your wife, Mrs. Canton. Not your mother." She giggled behind her hand, which was about the least remorseful thing

Matthew thought he'd ever seen. Although remorse for what, he still didn't know.

"You've lost me, Miss Timperman. Can you explain?"

"Oh!" Her face furrowed into one of sympathy—although it lasted maybe just a second or two. "I saw her with a man. I . . . thought you knew."

He narrowed his eyes at her as a horse and wagon lumbered by. Nothing in her expression indicated she thought he already knew. She was waiting for his reaction. "What man?" he said carefully.

"Oh, I don't know. He was tall. Portly." She shrugged as if it didn't matter at all. "It looked as if they knew each other well."

Matthew stared at her, alarm snaking its way through his body. The man who had come asking for him when he wasn't here fit that description. "Did she appear to be in distress?"

Miss Timperman shrugged. "I don't know. I don't think so? They looked . . . close." But she sounded far less sure of herself.

His eyes searched the street. A terrible feeling wound its way through every muscle and bone in his body. "Where did you see them? And when?"

"By the bank. I don't remember when. Matthew, if you don't trust Mrs. Canton, then perhaps . . ." She clasped her hands together. "Well, I feel terrible for suggesting such a thing, but I met an attorney who's only just arrived in town. I imagine he could take care of it for you."

Matthew stared at her, incredulous. He didn't have time for this nonsense, not if Sophia was in trouble. "By the bank," he repeated. And then something else occurred to him—something that made him go cold all over.

The man Sophia had feared was Francis Durham had been seen at the bank.

Miss Timperman appeared confused for a second, as if she'd expected him to up and agree to meet with this attorney immediately. "Yes, near the bank."

He ran a hand through his hair, his hat still inside the office. And without a word, he began to walk quickly in that direction.

"Matthew!" Miss Timperman's footsteps sound from behind him. "Please," she said when she caught up. "I think you ought to let them be."

He didn't answer her. Passing shops and empty lots and barely noticing a person he passed, Matthew moved as quickly as he could toward the far end of town. It couldn't be Durham . . . but it all felt far too coincidental for it *not* to be him.

He was desperate enough to come all the way to Colorado. And if he'd cornered Sophia . . . Matthew felt sick at the thought.

Miss Timperman scurried along after him, uttering protestations and pleas for him to stop. It made no sense, her desperate concern for him *not* to go after his wife. But he could worry about that later, once he'd found Sophia.

The bank had just come into view when he saw her. A man much larger than Sophia appeared plastered to her side. She was shaking her head as he reached for the door.

"Durham!" Matthew called.

The man whipped his head around, searching for the source of his name being spoken aloud. It *was* him, then. Matthew balled his fists and jogged ahead—just as Durham laid eyes on him. In a matter of seconds, the man slipped into the bank, dragging Sophia with him as she dropped her carpetbag.

"Matthew, please!" Miss Timperman grabbed hold of his arm as he reached the door. "Don't go in there. He's dangerous and he'll—he'll—"

Matthew paused, his hand on the door, and turned to look at the woman behind him. Suddenly, it all made sense. "You know him." He recoiled from her hand on his arm, shaking it off. "You're working with him."

She tucked her hands against her dress, her expression appropriately downcast. "It was wrong, I know that, but he promised . . . and I wanted . . ."

Matthew shook his head. He didn't have time for Miss Timperman's pathetic apologies, not while Sophia was in danger.

He went to yank open the door, only to find it locked. He banged on the door.

No answer.

Miss Timperman watched him, wide-eyed with one hand to her mouth as he backed away and circled around the building. There was a door in the rear, also locked.

One of the windows would have to do.

"What are you doing?" she asked as he grabbed a piece of wood from a pile nearby, which was likely waiting to be used in the building of a new shop or home.

Matthew didn't answer. He slammed the wood into the window, once, twice, three times—until the glass shattered. He shrugged off his jacket and wrapped it around his arm to clear away the remaining glass. Then, leaving Miss Timperman staring after him, he hoisted himself inside.

He found himself in an office. Weston Gardiner's, most likely, although the man himself wasn't present.

Everyone inside the bank must have heard the window breaking. Stealth was not on his side. And with that in mind, he shoved open the office door and entered the bank.

Chapter Twenty-five

"DURHAM!"

Sophia had never heard such a welcome voice in her life. She almost didn't believe it was him, until Mr. Durham turned, yanking her with him. And there he was—Matthew.

Behind him, Miss Timperman peaked through the open office door where Sophia supposed Matthew had entered by breaking the window they'd all heard shattering.

Durham shoved Sophia in front of him, that revolver pressed into her side.

"You stay right there," Mr. Durham said, a slight unease she hadn't heard before entering his voice. "Your wife was preparing to ask the clerk here to withdraw my money."

The poor bank teller, a small, thin man with an even skinnier mustache, had been the only person present in the bank when they'd entered. But bless him, he'd drawn himself up as tall as he could and insisted he could not take any money out of Sophia's account without her direct consent.

Which she hadn't given.

Across the room, Matthew raised his hands. "Did Mrs. Canton tell you she had only a paltry sum left?"

Sophia blinked at him. Certainly, she had much less than she'd started with, but what remained wasn't exactly "paltry."

Matthew was lying. His eyes flicked to hers, and she knew, in that moment, that he didn't hold the things he'd already forgiven her for against her.

She'd been wrong. And now it was too late.

Unless they could get out of here.

"She said she'd spent some. But I can tell with the hesitance she has to give me the rest that there is certainly plenty remaining."

"Oh, no," Sophia said, her voice stronger than she'd expected it to be. "It's just that it's *all* I have. Surely anyone would protect the little they have remaining to their name?"

His hand squeezed even harder around her arm. "You're lying."

"She's not," Matthew said.

Durham didn't speak for a moment, and Sophia prayed it was working. That he'd give up and leave.

"Then I want the land. What's left of the money *and* your land, Canton," Durham finally said.

"You can't have that!" Miss Timperman appeared from around the office door. "That's mine. Mine and Matthew's, when we marry. You promised me." She narrowed her eyes at Mr. Durham.

Sophia gaped at the woman's utter gall—both at stepping forward into this fray and at her continuing insistence that Matthew would marry her. And yet she almost felt bad for the woman at the same time. It was one thing to be jealous, and quite another to feel so desperate as to partner up with a man like Mr. Durham.

"What did he promise you?" Matthew asked, lowering his hands some.

When she didn't answer, Mr. Durham spoke up. "She thinks you'll marry her once your wife has nothing left to her name. Although it appears she already has nothing left . . . perhaps that's why she was headed out of town. You'd already sent her packing." The note of glee in Durham's voice grated on Sophia. How dare he presume such a thing?

"I did no such thing," Matthew said. "I don't know what Miss Timperman told you, but I certainly didn't marry Sophia for her money."

"*He* told me you would marry me once she lost her money." Miss Timperman pointed at Mr. Durham, who shrugged in response.

He didn't care a whit about Miss Timperman, that much was clear. Perhaps . . .

"Miss Timperman," Sophia said, desperate to pull away from Mr. Durham but not wanting to risk him using that gun. "Daisy." She tried to communicate with the other woman with her eyes, but Daisy's gaze swept from Sophia back to Mr. Durham.

"You promised me." Miss Timperman glared at Mr. Durham.

"I don't *care* what I told you," he said, sounding more exasperated at Miss Timperman than he had at Sophia's refusal to ask the bank clerk to withdraw her money. He turned back to Matthew. "After we finish here, we'll go to your office where you'll sign over that deed to me."

"Absolutely not," Matthew replied, his voice calm as could be. "Besides, what would you do with it? You don't strike me as a farmer or a ranching man."

Durham laughed. "Not a thing. I'll hold on to it, let it increase in value, and then sell it."

"That's *my* land," Miss Timperman said, her face going pink. "For me and the husband you'd promised I would have."

"He promised you something that won't happen," Matthew said.

Her face went an even darker pink. "I'm finished with this. With *all* of this. I hope you rot in your money and your land, Mr. Durham."

And with that, she stalked to the rear of the bank. A few seconds later, a door slammed shut.

"Good riddance," Mr. Durham said, yanking Sophia back around toward the clerk. "Now, where were we?"

"I'm not giving you my money." She tried to pull away and he shoved her against the counter. Her hip smarted with the contact, and the clerk winced in sympathy.

"Let her go." Matthew took a step forward, only for Mr. Durham to raise that pistol and point it directly at him.

"After I get my money and that deed. This is taking much too long. Now—"

But he didn't get to finish, because a commotion came from the rear of the building.

"The door," Durham said, a note of urgency in his voice, just as the bank filled with more men than Sophia had seen gathered in one place outside of the church.

Every single one of them held a weapon. The marshal, Mr. Gilbert, Mr. Gardiner, all of them, even Mr. Darby from the boarding house. And right there, bringing up the rear, was Miss Timperman, her arms crossed and a haughty smile plastered onto her face.

Chapter Twenty-six

IT WAS OVER IN AN INSTANT.

Durham hadn't put up a fight, not with that many guns trained on him. He'd shoved Sophia away, and Matthew caught her as the man tried to run. He got as far as the front door before Gilbert and Marshal Wright grabbed him. He was on his way to the jail now as Miss Timperman crowed to every person who passed by outside that she'd put an end to a bank robbery.

Of course, all she'd done was happen to exit the bank the same moment that the men Gilbert had rounded up after figuring out something was wrong had arrived. But it didn't matter. Sophia was safe, Miss Timperman seemed to finally understand that Matthew wouldn't marry her, and the specter of Mr. Durham was finally erased from the shadows.

Matthew walked Sophia home. She held tight to him, her anger at him vanished, and he hadn't let go of her for a second since Durham had turned her loose. When they reached the house, she asked if they might keep walking to the livery after she dropped off her carpetbag.

"I want to ride to the ranch," she said.

It was the first time either of them had referred to that empty piece of land as "the ranch," but he hoped with all his heart it wouldn't be the last. And so they did, after stopping by the marshal's office to tell him all that had happened before his arrival at the bank. Sophia had claimed innocence on behalf of Miss Timperman, which was more than the woman deserved.

"She made a terrible mistake," Sophia told him as they walked to the livery. "I imagine we won't see her at our doorstep anytime soon."

At the livery, Mrs. Carlisle made a fuss over Sophia as they waited for horses. She made Sophia promise to come for a visit as soon as she could, to which Sophia readily agreed. Matthew stood back and smiled at the exchange. Sophia had easily made friends with nearly every woman in town. She belonged here. With him.

If she'd forgiven him for not believing her.

They rode out of town, headed north with the mountains on either side of them. Matthew's stomach grumbled, and he realized it was past noon and neither of them had eaten. But Sophia looked unbothered, her face turned up to the sun and her eyes closed.

"I do love it here," she finally said.

"As do I." He waited for her to say something else, but she didn't. Not until they arrived.

He helped her off her horse and they stood there, on the land where he hoped to build a home.

"Sophia," he said, breaking the silence around them. "I am sorry for not taking to heart your concerns about Miss Timperman."

She nodded, not looking at him.

His heart ached, uncertain if she forgave him. Or if she still wished to leave. He couldn't hold her here if she did. And so he mustered all of his courage and put his thoughts into words. "I never once wished to marry her after I'd met you. I want you to know that. If you want to leave, I understand. But please leave knowing that I love you, and I won't stop just because you aren't here with me."

She turned to him then, tears brimming in her eyes. "Do you mean that?"

"I love you." He said the words again, even more fervently. "I've never known anything more certainly than I know that."

One tear fell, and he instinctively lifted a hand to brush it away.

She closed her eyes at his touch, and then they fluttered open again. "I love you, too, Matthew. I was afraid . . . well, I thought you hadn't ever really forgiven me for pretending to be someone else."

His heart ached that she'd thought such a thing. "I only held that against you for about ten minutes."

A smile traced her lips then. "That's a very short amount of time."

"And it's absolutely true." He swallowed, curling and uncurling his hands. "Does that mean you wish to stay?"

She nodded, and his heart leapt in joy. "I don't ever want to be anywhere without you," she said. "I only planned to leave because I thought you didn't want me."

"I want you, Sophia. More than anything." He closed the distance between them, unable to stay away from her any longer. He placed his hands on either side of her perfect, beautiful face as she tilted her head up.

"Will you finally kiss me now?"

He laughed, but only for a second, because he'd been waiting for that invitation for so long. He covered her mouth with his, gentle at first, until she wrapped her arms around him and pulled him closer.

And then everything fell away. There was no Durham or Miss Timperman, no deception, no money, no anything at all except for the two of them. She surrounded him and became part of his very being until he thought he couldn't breathe without her there.

When he tried to pull away, she drew him back, her sweet lips seeking his out again, until finally, both of them breathless, they drew apart.

He enveloped her in his arms, her back to his chest, as they looked over the land toward the mountains.

"Tell me," she said. "Will there be a porch on either side of the house so we can take in the sunrise and the sunset?"

"Of course. With rocking chairs."

"And chickens. Can we have chickens?" She tilted her head to look up at him, and Matthew thought he'd never seen anyone so enthused about chickens.

"Why not? We could keep goats too, if you wish. And a milk cow."

She smiled, content, and leaned back against him. "Then I believe I will remain married to you, Mr. Canton."

He threw back his head and laughed before turning her around to kiss her again.

Epilogue

ONE YEAR LATER . . .

Sophia stood with her hands on her hips, glaring at the milk cow.

"The chickens are easy. The goats love me. But you. You are one ornery creature," she said.

The cow stamped her hoof and lowed. Sophia shook her head. "I suppose I'll come back when you're in a better mood."

Milk cows, she'd thought, liked to be milked first thing in the morning. But not this one. She appeared to prefer breakfast and a little post-breakfast nap before a milking. Sophia hung the stool and stepped out into the cool of the morning.

Low clouds hung over the mountains to the west as the sun broke over the east.

Sophia laid a hand on her stomach as the baby kicked. She smiled at the movement. Nothing in life had prepared her for the wonder she felt at her own child coming to life inside her.

"It's going to be a beautiful morning." Matthew appeared from the barn, pulling off his gloves. He laid a hand on Sophia's stomach, and the baby kicked again. "This little one is lively today."

"Hungry, most likely," Sophia said. "The cow won't let me milk her, so I suppose I ought to feed both her and us."

"Are you ever giving that cow a name?"

Sophia lifted her chin. "She'll remain 'the cow' until she decides to be less particular about her milking schedule."

Matthew laughed. "And if the baby is the same, will he—or she—simply be 'the baby' until he's five years old?"

"If necessary," Sophia said with a smile.

He held out his arms and she willingly stepped into them. He ran one hand over her aching back as he held her to him. "Are you feeling well?"

"As well as I can be. But it isn't so terrible. I feel lucky, compared to some of the stories I've heard." She leaned back to look up at him. His jaw held more of a beard now that he'd been so busy with the ranch. She reached up a hand and ran her fingers over it. "Do you expect the cattle to arrive today?"

He nodded. "I've got a couple of men who've agreed to hire on. They should be here this afternoon to help."

"It's really happening," she said. "Everything we've talked about."

"It's happening." He drew her closer, trapping her hand against his face.

She smiled up at him. "Do you need help naming the cattle?"

He laughed.

"I'm very good at it. Let's see . . . Steer. Steer Number Two. Cow. Big Cow. Spotted Cow. Small—" He cut off her words with a kiss.

Sophia rested her hand against his face. The breeze lifted her hair as she kissed him back. He made a sound in the back of his throat, and she smiled against his lips.

When they finally parted, he said, his voice a little ragged, "You can name the cattle and all our children whatever you like provided you kiss me like that until the day we die."

"Agreed," she said with a laugh.

And then she kissed him again under the sky and with all the land that was theirs and theirs alone surrounding them.

She would have braved another wagon train, ten more ladies just like Miss Timperman, and a hundred bands of outlaws for him and for this life.

And she knew he'd do the same. They were family and nothing would ever pull them apart.

THANK YOU FOR READING! I hope you enjoyed Matthew and Sophia's story. The next book in the series, *A Sheriff's Bride*[1], is available to pre-order now. That book finds the new sheriff of the Crest Stone's brand new county in need of a wife—a wife he doesn't think he wants, until she arrives.

Want to know how the little town of Crest Stone began? Find out in the Gilbert Girls series. The first book in that series is *Building Forever*[2].

To be alerted about my new books, sign up here: http://bit.ly/catsnewsletter I give subscribers a free download of *Forbidden Forever*, a Gilbert Girls prequel novella. You'll also get sneak peeks at upcoming books, insights into the writer life, discounts and deals, inspirations, and so much more. I'd love to have *you* join the fun!

Turn the page to see a complete list of my books.

1. *https://amzn.to/3z0PWPr*

2. *http://bit.ly/BuildingForeverbook*

More Books by Cat Cahill

Crest Stone Mail-Order Brides **series**

A Hopeful Bride[1]

A Rancher's Bride[2]

A Bartered Bride[3]

A Sheriff's Bride[4]

The Gilbert Girls **series**

Building Forever[5]

Running From Forever[6]

Wild Forever[7]

Hidden Forever[8]

Forever Christmas[9]

On the Edge of Forever[10]

---

1. https://bit.ly/HopefulBride
2. http://bit.ly/RanchersBride
3. https://bit.ly/barteredbride
4. https://amzn.to/3z0PWPr
5. http://bit.ly/BuildingForeverbook
6. http://bit.ly/RunningForeverBook
7. http://bit.ly/WildForeverBook
8. http://bit.ly/HiddenForeverBook
9. http://bit.ly/ForeverChristmasBook

The Gilbert Girls Book Collection – Books 1-3[11]

The Gilbert Girls Book Collection – Books 4-6[12]

***Brides of Fremont County* series**

Grace[13]

Molly[14]

Ruthann[15]

Norah[16]

Charlotte (part of the Secrets, Scandals, & Seduction boxset)[17]

Other Sweet Historical Western Romances by Cat

***The Proxy Brides* series**

A Bride for Isaac [18]

A Bride for Andrew [19]

A Bride for Weston[20]

***The Blizzard Brides* series**

A Groom for Celia [21]

A Groom for Faith[22]

---

10. http://bit.ly/EdgeofForever
11. http://bit.ly/GilbertGirlsBox
12. https://amzn.to/3gYPXcA
13. http://bit.ly/ConfusedColorado
14. https://bit.ly/DejectedDenver
15. https://bit.ly/brideruthann
16. https://amzn.to/3IyJRuA
17. https://books2read.com/u/4joPNj
18. http://bit.ly/BrideforIsaac
19. https://bit.ly/BrideforAndrew
20. https://bit.ly/BrideforWeston
21. http://bit.ly/GroomforCelia
22. http://bit.ly/GroomforFaith

A Groom for Josie[23]

Last Chance Brides **series**

A Chance for Lara[24]

The Matchmaker's Ball **series**

Waltzing with Willa[25]

Westward Home and Hearts Mail-Order Brides **series**

Rose's Rescue[26]

Matchmaker's Mix-Up **series**

William's Wistful Bride[27]

Ransom's Rowdy Bride[28]

The Sheriff's Mail-Order Bride **series**

A Bride for Hawk[29]

Keepers of the Light **series**

The Outlaw's Promise[30]

Mail-Order Brides' First Christmas **series**

A Christmas Carol for Catherine[31]

The Broad Street Boarding House **series**

Starla's Search[32]

---

23. https://bit.ly/GroomforJosie
24. https://amzn.to/3sAj0IV
25. https://bit.ly/WaltzingwithWilla
26. https://bit.ly/RoseRescue
27. https://bit.ly/WilliamsWistfulBride
28. https://amzn.to/3s0Lqwq
29. https://bit.ly/BrideforHawk
30. https://bit.ly/OutlawsPromise
31. https://bit.ly/ChristmasCarolCatherine
32. https://amzn.to/32sQuPS

About the Author, Cat Cahill

A SUNSET. SNOW ON THE mountains. A roaring river in the spring. A man and a woman who can't fight the love that pulls them together. The danger and uncertainty of life in the Old West. This is what inspires me to write. I hope you find an escape in my books!

I live with my family and a houseful of dogs and cats in Kentucky. When I'm not writing, I'm losing myself in a good book, planning my next travel adventure, doing a puzzle, attempting to garden, or wrangling my kids.

Made in the USA
Monee, IL
08 March 2023